Demon Revealed

Book 2 of the Demon Cursed Series

SADIE HOBBES

Scottish Seoul Publishing, LLC

ALSO BY SADIE HOBBES

The Demon Cursed Series
Demon Cursed
Demon Revealed
Demon Heir

The Four Kingdoms Series
Order of the Goddess

CHAPTER 1

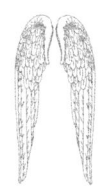

ADDIE

"Look!"

I didn't know who had called out. But all eyes around me turned up. The same bright light that had appeared just minutes ago was now disappearing into the sky. Did that mean the threat was over?

The residents of Sterling Peak didn't seem to think so. More and more of them streamed out of their homes. Those racing up the hill tended to be younger, stronger. Most of them were Rangers of the Seraph Force, the security force that protected the people of Sterling Peak from demon attacks. They had only recently extended that protection to the people across the bridge in Blue Forks.

I knew they had no idea what they were racing toward. From down the hill, all they would have been able to see was a rapidly descending ball of light. They had no way of knowing that it was the arrival, and now the departure, of the archangel Michael.

But I knew.

I kept the hood of my cloak up, my long dark hair tucked

underneath. I dropped my chin whenever I spied a Ranger, praying none of them recognized me.

I slipped behind a group of six people, all staff from one of the higher houses.

"What do you think that was?" a woman with bright-red hair cut short asked.

A man with gray hair glanced over his shoulder, his brown eyes worried. "It has to be some sort of new demon attack."

It was not a surprising guess. The archangel's appearance right on the heels of a ferocious demon attack was not something anyone would guess. After all, no one had seen an angel in over a hundred years.

When I had first seen the ball of light, I'd been terrified. But fear had turned into awe as the archangel Michael stepped from the glowing light.

But that fear shifted once again to terror as the archangel Michael reached out for Graham and removed his free will, making him the archangel's tool.

The group in front of me slipped down a separate road, heading toward the theater. I continued on toward Celestial bridge, even though everything in me rebelled and wanted to head back up the hill, back to Graham.

For the first time in the two years since I'd woken up on that beach, I had felt safe, which was crazy because I had just fought off a demon attack.

But it wasn't the physical harm that had ever been a problem. I had been fighting demons every night since. The difference was now, I felt like the kids and I weren't alone. We had people in our lives looking out for us, who cared about us. And walking away from that was just so incredibly hard. But to keep them safe, I needed to keep them away from me. I needed to go.

Because if Marcus was right, Graham would be looking for me.

To kill me.

I still struggled with that idea. I'd thought Marcus was crazy when he'd first relayed it. But there had been something about Graham, a coldness in him after the archangel had encapsulated him in light.

A man bumped into me. "Sorry, sorry," he panted.

I didn't even have time to respond before he slipped through the crowd. Everyone was terrified. And so was I.

Not just because of the prophecy that Marcus had told me about. But because Marcus had finally figured out who my father was. And that revelation drove terror straight through my heart.

Because I was the daughter of an archangel, all right, but that archangel was Lucifer.

My skin crawled at the idea. Since I'd woken up on the beach two years earlier, I'd been trying to figure out who I was. I had no memory of my time before the beach.

But in my wildest dreams or nightmares, I never imagined this. Just a few hours ago, I thought my life was on a trajectory that would bring me everything I had ever wanted: a safe home for myself, Noel, and Micah; new friends like Donovan, Tess, Marcus, and Laura; and a new job, if I wanted it, with the Seraph Force that would actually provide me with a livable wage.

And I had Graham.

For the first time in my life, I felt powerful. I'd just discovered that I actually had wings that I could call upon at will. And the wings became enflamed when I needed them to. It was the best discovery of my life.

When the demon horde had reached Blue Forks, I'd been able to fight them off. And I had been exhilarated about it. I knew that was what I was born to do. I'd protected the people of Blue Forks and the people of Sterling Peak. I'd returned to Graham's home content, despite the horror of what I'd been through. I knew my purpose in life: to protect people.

And I knew that I wanted Graham to be part of that future.

In one fell swoop, Marcus's revelations had ripped all of that away. According to the prophecy, I was destined to fight Graham. With Graham's free will removed, he would fight me to the death. But I can't say the same. I know I would never be able to look into his eyes and watch the life drain from them. There was no way I would be able to kill him.

So instead I ran. I just needed to figure out where I was running to.

CHAPTER 2

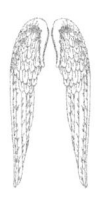

NOEL

Fourteen-year-old Noel Rikbiel hurried down the hill toward the bridge. Next to her, Micah Rikbiel cast a glance over his shoulder.

"Don't look," Noel said.

Micah turned his gaze back to her.

She forced a smile to her face. "Addie will be okay."

"What do you think that was?" he asked.

Noel shook her head, clasping his hand more securely. She had no answer beyond the obvious: trouble.

She'd seen the light in the sky. At first she'd thought it was a meteor. But then it had slowed. She'd wanted to argue with Addie when she told them to find Lieutenant Commander Donovan Gabriel, second-in-command of the Seraph Force, but something deep and primal inside of her told her to get Micah away from that light.

It was an old reflex, one Noel had felt deep inside her ever since they'd first met in that horrible orphanage six years ago. He'd been so small, smaller than the other kids his age. She, at least, had been hardened, even at that young an age. But Micah, at age six, could still be shocked by the cruelty in the world. And therefore he was completely unprepared for it.

Protecting him had been her job ever since. Then two years ago, Addie had shown up, and she looked out for both of them. Rarely did Addie need looking after. But Noel worried that right now she might be up against something stronger than even her.

Noel had grabbed Micah's hand to run, expecting a massive explosion. But there'd been nothing. She didn't know what that meant. She didn't know if she should allow herself the luxury of thinking everything was all right.

Micah's dark-brown eyes looked up at her with complete trust. "We should be with Addie."

Noel shook her head. Everything in her told her to run a little faster. "No. Whatever she's handling, we'd just be in the way."

"We're not in the way."

Noel winced, realizing how harsh her words had come out. "Not like that. Addie will always be on our side. But if she has to fight or help people, you know she would be looking out for us first instead of herself. And then she could end up getting hurt. Let's just find Donovan, okay?"

"There he is." Micah pointed toward the bridge.

The Celestial Bridge connected Sterling Peak to Blue Forks. Built at the end of the Angel War, it had been created from stone and steel. Standing on its highest point, looking out over Blue Forks, were statues of the archangels Michael and Gabriel, as if keeping an eye on them. But the bridge's most prominent feature belied that suggestion: the bridge could be retracted to protect the residents of Sterling Peak from a demon attack. The fact that such an action left the residents of Blue Forks at the mercy of the demons hadn't been much of a consideration to the residents of Sterling Peak.

At least until recently, until Graham had started to change things.

Noel still didn't know what to think of Graham. She liked him, and he seemed to be trying to do the right thing, but Noel's trust was hard won, and she wasn't ready to give it, not quite yet.

But she was still worried about him. She hoped both he and Addie would be okay. Because Graham was a lot like Addie: he would put other people's safety well before his own.

Although the bridge was crowded with anxious people, it was easy to pick out Donovan. He stood head and shoulders above all the other people there. His dark hair had come loose from his ponytail, and his face looked unusually serious. Noel had never really seen Donovan look serious. She knew he was the lieutenant commander of the Seraph Force, but whenever she or Micah saw him, he was smiling and telling them some ridiculous story. But right now, there was nothing ridiculous about his mood.

And that made Noel feel better.

He walked with Sheila Castiel, the head of bridge security. Noel frowned when she noticed the limp.

"He's hurt." Micah pulled his hand from hers and darted ahead, slipping more easily through the crowds due to his smaller size.

"Micah!" Noel picked up her pace, trying to keep up with him. He'd just reached the edge of the bridge when she caught him.

"Donovan," Micah called.

Donovan turned around. Looks of surprise splashed across both his and Sheila's faces. "What are you two doing here?" Donovan asked as he waved them forward. The guards at the bridge stepped back, allowing them entrance.

Donovan looked back toward the hill. "Were you at Graham's house?"

Noel nodded. Donovan pulled Noel and Micah a short distance away from the crowd, lowering his voice. "Does Addie know where you are? She was heading to Graham's house."

"We saw her. She told us to run as soon as she saw that light," Noel said.

"What is it?" Micah asked.

Donovan narrowed his eyes, his gaze going to the top of the hill. "I don't know. Tess and a bunch of the others went to go check it out."

"How come you didn't go with them?" Micah asked.

Donovan blew out a breath, running a hand through his hair. "Two reasons. One, right now I am in charge while Graham's healing, and two, this stupid ankle makes me slow. I sent half of the Seraph Force up to see what was going on. But I need to keep the other half down here to keep on guard for the demons."

"But Addie said they were gone," Noel said.

"And I hope she's right. But we need to keep watch, just in case."

Noel looked back toward the hill, not happy at how quiet it was. "Addie told us to come stay with you. She didn't want us to be anywhere near that light."

Donovan stared off in the distance again. Then he met Noel's gaze. And for a split second, she saw his concern. Then he seemed to shake himself from his musing. He looked at Micah and grinned. "We can always use an extra pair of eyes on the bridge."

He glanced at Noel. "Or two."

Noel felt her cheeks flush. Donovan always had that effect on her. She knew her crush was crazy. He was way out of her league. Her body, though, didn't seem to want to listen to that.

"Come on. I'll put you two to work."

CHAPTER 3

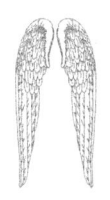

ADDIE

Up ahead, I could see the bridge. The crowd parted as a group of Seraph Force soldiers appeared. I ducked my head as they sprinted past me. But I caught sight of Major Tess Uriel, one of the Seven, at the head of the group. I clamped my mouth shut to keep myself from calling out to her. She was a friend. She would help if I asked her to.

But I couldn't put her in the middle of this. If Marcus was right, Graham would kill anyone who got in between us.

Once the group had passed, I continued onward, careful to keep my eyes searching the crowd for anyone I knew. I couldn't be recognized. Luckily, the darkness helped with that. Although every light in Sterling Peak seemed to be on. Ahead, I saw a familiar snatch of dark hair in the bright lights of the bridge. Donovan stood speaking with someone. The crowd shifted, and I saw Noel. My heart lurched.

I searched the crowd and saw Micah just a few feet away. My steps slowed at the sight of the two of them. How could I leave them? They were my family. Maybe I didn't have to. Maybe I could bring them with me. Maybe—

The screech of a horn cut off my thoughts. A man next to me pulled me out of the road as a car sped by. I stumbled over my feet, nearly face-planting onto the sidewalk.

"Watch out." The man held on to me, making sure I was secure before he released me.

I nodded my thanks, keeping my face turned away. "Thanks."

"Be careful out there," he said by way of farewell.

I barely heard him, my gaze focused on the car that sped down the road. Cars were rarely used in Sterling Peak. They were rarely used at all in this new world.

But I knew that car. It was Graham's.

The car slammed to a stop at the edge of the bridge's barriers. Graham stepped out, casting a look around. I hunched my shoulders and moved with the slower pace of an older person, careful to keep my head down, while watching him from the corner of my eyes. His gaze slipped right over me. Then he abruptly turned and marched toward Donovan.

I made my way closer to the bridge, keeping an eye on the two of them. Donovan's face shifted from a look of concern to one of confusion as they talked. Donovan crossed his arms over his chest, shaking his head as he glared at Graham.

Graham went to step around Donovan, but Donovan held out his arm, keeping him back. Graham pushed Donovan's arm away and slammed his fist into the side of Donovan's face.

My jaw dropped.

Donovan's face reflected my own shock. I couldn't believe what I was witnessing. Donovan was the closest person on this planet to Graham. An hour ago, the idea of him hitting Donovan was completely unbelievable, especially for something so small.

Yet a lot had changed in a very short time.

That action brought home the truth. Graham was no longer Graham. Marcus was right.

Which meant I needed to get as far away from here as possible before anyone else got hurt.

CHAPTER 4

NOEL

Noel's nerves were stretched tight. She kept looking back toward the top of the hill. The glow that had been there had long since disappeared. But she couldn't stop the feeling that something horrible had just happened.

Yet no noise came from up the hill. There were no screams, no cries. Everything was silent.

More and more residents of Sterling Peak streamed down the hill toward the bridge. Obviously they had seen the light and wanted to get as far from it as possible. The problem was that the only place to go *was* the bridge. Yet no one wanted to cross it because they hadn't checked Blue Forks yet to make sure that the demons were completely gone. They were waiting until morning. Which meant that the area around the bridge was completely packed with people.

"Tell Mrs. Uriel that I am not going to clear a section for the Angel Blessed," Donovan growled. "She wants her own space, tell her to go back to her damn house."

Major Laura Raguel stood next to him, an eyebrow raised. "I'm guessing you want me to put that in my own words."

"Your words, my words, I don't give a damn." He took a breath, running a hand through his hair before he closed his eyes and pinched the bridge of his nose. "Okay, on second thought, use your words."

Laura smiled and then slapped him on the back. "Don't worry. Graham will be down here soon, and all of this misery will be just a memory."

"God, I hope so," Donovan mumbled. Then he caught Noel watching him. He gave her a shrug. "I'm not great at being political. Graham is much better at it than me."

Noel grinned. "Yeah, I kind of noticed. You're more of a hammer."

Donovan's face lit up. "That's the nicest thing anybody's ever said to me."

Noel laughed out loud despite her nerves.

Her laugh elicited a wider smile from Donovan. Then his smile dimmed. He glanced back up the hill. It had been fifteen minutes since the light appeared and then disappeared again. A group of Seraph Force had gone up to see what was going on, but none of them had returned yet.

"No word?" Noel asked.

Donovan shook his head. "You know what they say, no news is good news."

Noel nodded, but she actually did it more to make Donovan feel better than because she believed him. Besides, she had the distinct impression he didn't believe his words either.

Movement from the corner of her eye caught her attention. She turned her head, looking through the crowd. A face turned away, their head covered in a cloak. Noel watched them go with a frown. Strange.

"Finally," Donovan growled.

He started toward the main entrance of the bridge.

Noel glanced over at where Micah was standing with Sheila's sister, Marjorie. He'd be good for a few minutes. She hurried after Donovan.

As soon as she broke free of some of the crowd, she realized what had caught Donovan's eyes. Graham strode out from a car, twelve Seraph Force Rangers spread out behind him.

Noel smiled, relief filling her at the sight of him. Graham was in one piece. That was a good—

But Noel's steps faltered as she took in his face. Something was different. He looked so serious. And where was Addie?

She picked up her pace again, but not right next to Donovan, not sure if she would be ushered away, being this was probably Seraph Force business. But she knew how to be around and not be noticed. She slipped in next to one of Rangers so that she couldn't be seen by Graham or Donovan.

Graham marched up to Donovan and then stopped. "Have you seen Addison?"

Addison? No one called her Addison.

Donovan frowned. "No. I thought she was up at your house."

"I need everyone here searched. I need Addison found and brought to me." Graham's tone was harsh. Noel peeked around the Seraph Force in front of her to get a look at Graham's face. His eyes were narrowed, his jaw set. He looked angry. What the heck was going on?

Donovan's eyes narrowed as he looked at the Seraph Force surrounding them and then back at Graham. "Can I talk to you privately for a moment?"

Graham shook his head and started to walk past him. "No. Find Addison."

Donovan put out his arm, blocking his way. "What's going on, Graham? Why are you looking for—"

Graham's fist came up and slammed into the side of Donovan's face. Donovan turned his head at the last moment, escaping the full force of the hit. "What the hell, man?"

"You've been given an order. Find Addison Baker. You're the second-in-command. That means you *follow* my orders. If you can't do that, then you will be removed from your position."

Noel's mouth fell open as she stared at the two of them. What had gotten into Graham? Hitting Donovan? Threatening his removal?

Something was seriously wrong.

CHAPTER 5

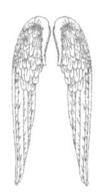

ADDIE

My heart pounded. Everything in me told me to go back, to get Noel and Micah. But would I be able to protect them from Graham? If he came for me, would they just get caught in between?

He had hit Donovan.

Donovan.

Marcus was right. No one would be off-limits when Graham came for me. Which meant Noel and Micah needed to be as far from me as humanly possible.

I turned, my whole body shaking as I moved along the edge of the bridge's foundation. No one paid any attention to me as I slipped along the path that edged along the river.

The water churned and rolled below me. I had always loved looking at the water, but right now, it seemed angry. The whole world seemed angry.

I forced my gaze away from it. I kept my shoulders hunched as I moved quickly away from the bridge and prying eyes. The lights along the path ended about a hundred yards from the bridge. I continued in the dark another two hundred yards, not wanting to take any chances. The river curved. I could only make out the top of the bridge, so I was sure no one would be able to see me.

I perched on the edge of the cliff, staring down. Was I really going to do this? Was I really going to leave everything I knew behind?

The cold look in Graham's eyes wafted through my mind. I straightened my shoulders, dropping the cloak. Whatever the archangel had done to him had removed the Graham I knew. And I needed to leave to keep those I cared about safe.

My wings burst out from my back without my flames. Taking a deep breath, I plunged off the cliff, skimming near the water as I made my way to the other side, praying that one day I would be able to make my way back.

CHAPTER 6

NOEL

Noel slipped away from the Seraph Force. She didn't know what exactly was going on, but the idea that Graham was looking for "Addison" did not sit well with her.

And if he was looking for Addie, it wouldn't be too long until he started to look for her and Micah.

Noel scanned the crowd. She moved to the spot where she had last seen Micah, but he was no longer there. She turned around, frantically looking for him. Then she heard Marjorie's laugh. She turned to the right and saw that the group had moved a little farther down the bank. They'd been partially hidden by some trees. She hurried down the path toward them. The group knelt down at the edge of the cliff, chucking rocks into the water.

Micah bent down to grab another rock, but Noel grabbed his arm and hauled him up. "Micah. Come on."

He frowned as he straightened. "What's going on?"

"We need to go."

He opened his mouth to reply, but then took in her face. He immediately dropped his rock. "Okay."

They dashed up the path, but when they reached the top, Noel put out her hand to slow him. They couldn't draw attention to themselves.

"What's going on?" Micah whispered.

"We need to get to the other side of the bridge. Something's going on with Addie. I don't know what. But I don't think it's good."

Micah looked up at her. "Donovan—"

"Can't help us. It's Graham who's looking for Addie. And something's wrong with him. We need to go now."

Micah opened his mouth to ask more questions but then shut it again, looking around uneasily as well.

Noel scanned the area, looking to see where Micah and Graham were. She couldn't see either of them.

But there was a line of Seraph Force guarding the bridge. They were going to have to somehow figure out a way to slip by them. "Look, we need to find a way past the guards. Damn, I wish Torr were here."

"So do I." Graham stepped from behind the crowd and in front of them. Noel's mouth dropped open and she turned to run but two Rangers appeared from behind them. They grabbed their arms.

Graham smiled. The smile held no warmth. "I need to ask you two some questions."

CHAPTER 7

ADDIE

As I FLEW, I tensed, waiting for someone to call out my name. But the world was silent.

When I reached the other side of the river, I stayed low, continuing to fly because I needed to be fast. But I also needed to make one more stop.

Blue Forks was deserted. All the residents had rushed across the bridge into Sterling Peak at the first sign of the demons. They would stay there until morning, after the Seraph Force made sure it was safe.

But some would be staying across the bridge a little longer. More than a few homes had been destroyed in the demons' rampage. It would take a while to rebuild. The old Graham would have made rebuilding a priority. I didn't know what the new Graham would prioritize.

There was one person, though, that I knew was still here.

I retracted my wings and touched down in the alley outside my old apartment building.

The building had been left over from the Before. It was an

actual building made of bricks. The paint was peeling on the walls, but the electricity and plumbing worked.

I'd been so proud the day I brought Noel and Micah here. And they'd been ecstatic about having their own rooms. The memory left me shaky, homesick, and worried that I wouldn't be able to add any more memories like that for a while.

I hurried down the alley and slipped in the front door. The door at the top of the stairs opened almost as soon as I stepped into the foyer. "Addie?"

Torr stood at the top of the stairs. He was four feet tall with a strong muscular build, with mottled green skin like all the other demons. I'd met Torr shortly after I'd woken up on that beach. Only recently, though, had he made his presence known to anyone else.

After the attack, he'd decided to stay in Blue Forks, not wanting to risk anyone catching sight of him across the bridge and setting off a panic. Now he peered down at me, a confused look on his face. "What are you doing here?"

I hurried up the stairs and stepped past him, closing the apartment door behind the two of us. Then I leaned against it. My shoulders slumped. I suddenly felt exhausted. It was nearing dawn, and I hadn't slept in close to twenty-four hours, plus the last few hours had been a little tiring.

Torr stepped back, staring at me. "Addie?"

I shook my head and cleared my throat. I could be tired later. Right now, I needed to explain to Torr what was happening and get moving.

He stared at me, his blue eyes filled with concern. My chest tightened. God, it had been so much easier in my mind. "I, uh, I came to say goodbye."

Torr went still and then spoke slowly. "What are you talking about?"

I sank onto the couch. "A lot's happened."

"A lot? You left me like thirty minutes ago. How much could have possibly happened?"

I wanted to laugh and cry at the same time. "You'd be surprised."

Taking a deep breath, I explained about Archangel Michael, Graham's transformation, and Marcus's warning.

"Are you sure?"

I pictured Graham's face, the stillness that had come over him. "I'm sure. If I stay, the people with me will be put in danger. Something's happened to Graham. He's not Graham, not anymore. He punched Donovan at the bridge."

Torr's mouth fell open. "What?"

"Donovan tried to get him to stop, and I think talk to him. Without warning, Graham punched him."

Torr stared at me for a long moment. I tensed, waiting for his arguments about why I shouldn't go. But he didn't offer any. "Where are you going to go?"

"I don't know."

And I didn't. I'd never been outside of Blue Forks besides going down to the docks and the small town of Nichols Inlet. Forks was located in an area that used to be Los Angeles. West was out because it ran right into the ocean. I shrugged. "I guess east."

"I'm going with you."

My head jerked up, alarm flashing through me. "No, no, I need you to stay here. I need you to tell Noel and Micah what happened."

This time it was Torr who shook his head. "Addie, you can't go by yourself. I know about your powers, but you're still going to need some help. Donovan, Tess, and Marcus will look out for Noel and Micah. Who's going to look out for you?"

"I'll be okay. It's not safe for you."

Torr gave a small laugh. "Addie, I'm a demon living in the

human world. There *is* no safe for me. And I can't let you go on your own. I'm coming."

For a moment, I thought maybe I should just leave now. If I took off into the air, he'd never be able to catch me. He'd never be able to track me.

But I didn't want to go alone. Maybe it was selfish, but I wanted someone to be with me. And Torr could stay invisible when he wanted to. It would offer him some protection.

"Okay. But we need to leave now."

CHAPTER 8

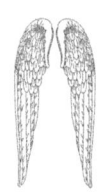

NOEL

GRAHAM HAD an armed escort bring Noel and Micah to the security shed next to the bridge. As they walked, Noel craned her head, looking for Donovan, Tess, Sheila, or anyone she knew, but she didn't see any of them.

"Eyes forward," Graham barked.

Noel's gaze shot to him, her eyes narrowing. But she held her tongue, not sure how he'd respond.

Graham pushed open the door to the shed. It was a single-story gray building that held a desk, a small cot, a few chairs, a small bathroom, and a cell along the back wall. The security officer at the desk jumped to his feet, a piece of a sandwich falling from his mouth. "Commander Michael."

"Out," was Graham's only response.

The man looked between all of us and then grabbed the other half of his sandwich and hightailed it for the door. Graham shut it after him. The Rangers who'd accompanied them were still outside. Noel hoped that was a good sign and not because Graham didn't want any witnesses.

Noel moved to the far side of the room, taking Micah with her and pulling him behind her.

Graham looked over at her and smiled. "You have nothing to fear from me. I'm your friend."

Every hair on Noel's body that stood at attention argued the exact opposite. And she believed those hairs over the words of the man standing in front of her. This Graham was most definitely not her friend.

The door opened behind Graham. Donovan and Tess slipped inside. Both of their gazes shifted from Graham to both kids. She could see their relief when they saw there were no new injuries on either of them. It wasn't comforting that they thought Graham was someone *capable* of hurting them. She'd hoped when he'd grabbed them that maybe it was her misgivings about Graham or just her paranoia going into overdrive.

Apparently not.

Graham looked over his shoulder at Donovan and Tess with a glare. "Do not interfere."

Donovan narrowed his eyes at Graham but nodded. Tess looked like she wanted to throttle him, but she nodded as well.

As soon as Graham turned his back to them, however, Donovan gave Noel a wink. She felt better immediately. Whatever was going on with Graham, it didn't change how Donovan felt about them. He wouldn't let any harm come to them.

"Now, why don't you two take a seat?" Graham pushed a chair toward Noel and carried another over and placed it next to it. He even wiped it off and then patted the seat. "Here you go, Micah."

Noel could see the fear in Micah's eyes, but she gave him a nod as she sat down. He sat right next to her.

"See? Isn't that better? Now we can have a nice conversation." Graham leaned back against the desk, striking what Noel thought was supposed to be a casual posture. But if anything, it signaled the exact opposite. His positioning made it clear just how rigid his whole body was at this moment. He looked like he was about to pounce.

Noel swallowed, knowing who would be on the receiving of that bit of brutality. And she reeled at the thought. Ever since they had come to Sterling Peak, Graham had been nothing but kind. He had provided them a home. He had taken care of their injuries. He had even kept Torr hidden. Where was *that* guy? Was he the real Graham, or was this guy in front of them the true Graham?

Her gaze shifted over to Donovan and Tess. Both of them looked at Graham with a combination of concern and anger. They seemed just as confused by the shift in Graham's personality as she was. So obviously if he had fooled her, he had fooled them for even longer. Years, in fact. So one thing was clear: whatever was going on with Graham right now, it was new to all of them.

"Now, when was the last time you saw Addison?" Graham asked.

Noel frowned. There was no point in lying about that. "Back at your house. Right before that big giant ball of light appeared in the sky."

Graham raised an eyebrow. "Addison was there for that?"

"She'd just gotten back. We met her by the front gate. We'd just asked her about what happened, and we were heading back into the house to see you..."

Noel paused. They'd been heading to the kitchen to check on Graham and his shoulder. She'd seen him when he first arrived. His face had been pale and etched in pain. But there was no evidence of that injury right now. She frowned. "Your shoulder. You were hurt."

Graham rolled his shoulder. "Not anymore. Now, you headed to the house and..."

Noel shook herself from trying to figure out how his shoulder had healed. "Uh, we saw the light, like I said. Addie pulled us to a stop. She told us to run and find Donovan."

Graham nodded. "Is that what you did?"

"Yes. Because if Addie tells us to do something, it's for our own good, our safety. So we came down to the bridge to find Donovan."

Tess stepped forward. "I passed them when I was on the way up to your house. They're telling the truth."

Graham looked over at Tess. Noel couldn't decipher the look on his face. He turned back to Noel and Micah. "I see. And you haven't seen her since then?"

"She was supposed to be with you," Noel said. "She was going to see how you were doing. You know, after she saved you and everybody else from the demon horde."

Graham smiled again, but again, the smile held no warmth. "She did indeed save everyone. Did you ever wonder how?"

Noel frowned. "What do you mean how? She fought them off."

"That's part of the story. But not all of it."

Noel flicked a glance at Donovan before focusing back on Graham. "What are you talking about?"

Graham ignored the question. "How long did you speak with Addison?"

"A minute? Maybe two?" Noel said, not sure what Graham was getting at.

He leaned further back. "Where would she go if she were on the run?"

"On the run?" Noel asked. "Why would she be on the run? She's a hero."

"Where would she go?" Graham repeated.

Noel stared at him. Graham moved incredibly fast. He grabbed Micah and pushed him up against the wall, his knife at his neck. Donovan and Tess bolted from their positions toward him. Graham pushed the knife deeper into Micah's neck, and he turned Micah so he was in front of him. Micah let out a little cry.

Tess and Donovan stopped, their fists clenched.

"What are you doing?" Tess demanded.

"Getting answers," Graham said.

Anger raced through Noel at the fear on Micah's face. "Let. Him. Go."

"Where would she go?" Graham pushed the knife deeper. A spot of blood appeared.

Micah trembled. "I don't know. The apartment. Blue Forks. She's never been anywhere else. Except down to the docks once to get medicine for someone. Blue Forks is all she knows."

Graham stared at Noel, his face almost pleasant as a small trail of blood reached Micah's shirt. "What about her life before two years ago? Has she told you anything about that?"

Noel wanted to kill him. He asked the question so casually while threatening Micah just as casually. And he knew the answer to that question. Noel's voice shook with a combination of fear and rage. "She doesn't remember anything from before she woke up on the beach. You *know* that."

Graham leaned down to Micah's ear. "What about you, Micah? Do you know anything about her life before? Has she let slip any information?"

Micah was shaking so hard that it made his words hard to decipher. "No. She's never said anything. She doesn't go anywhere. She goes to work. She patrols Blue Forks. That's it. There are no other places she would go."

Graham backed away from Micah, sliding his knife into his sheath. He gave Micah a small shove. Tess grabbed him and pulled him behind her.

Graham smiled. "I'm sorry about the unpleasantness. But it was necessary to make sure that you are telling the truth. You are very attached to her, and therefore your words couldn't be trusted."

Noel rushed over to Micah and pulled him into her arms. He clung to her, his whole body shaking. Noel just glared back at Graham. "Apology not accepted."

Graham inclined his head toward her. "Equally understandable. You two will be escorted back to my home. You will remain there until Addison has been retrieved."

"Graham, what is going on?" Tess demanded.

"We need to find Addison Baker. She is a grave threat to everyone in Sterling Peak. That is all you need to know." Graham strode to the door and flung it open, speaking to the guards outside. "Take them back to my home. And establish two guards to watch them at all times."

Three Rangers stepped inside as Graham disappeared outside. Noel didn't recognize any of them. Donovan glared at the men. "We will take them back to Graham's home. You are not needed."

One of the Rangers shook his head, shooting a nervous glance back at the door. "The commander—"

"Did not realize that we would take them. Go find something else to do," Donovan ordered.

The three men looked at one another and then backed out of the room, closing the door behind them. Donovan turned to Noel and Micah. His voice was rough. "Are you two all right?"

Noel took the edge of her sleeve and pressed it against the cut at Micah's neck. "Are you okay?"

He pushed away her hand, but Noel could feel his fear. "I'm fine. Quit it."

"What the hell is going on?" Tess demanded. "What was all that? Has Graham lost his damn mind?"

"That's the question, isn't it?" Donovan looked at Tess. "We are not leaving Noel and Micah in his care. You, me, or Laura must be at Graham's home while Noel and Micah are there. I don't know what's going on with Graham, but I don't trust him."

"Donovan," Tess began, a warning in her tone.

Donovan speared her with a look. "If I told you two days ago that Graham would threaten a child's life to get information, would you have believed me?"

Tess stared at him for a moment and then shook her head.

"Me either. But he just did. Something is going on with

Graham. And until we find out what it is, none of us can trust him."

Donovan looked over at Noel. "And if push comes to shove, we'll get you to out of there. But for right now, we need to play along with whatever game Graham is playing. We need to find out what his angle is. We need to find out why he's looking for Addie."

Noel nodded, knowing there was no other course at hand. If they took off right now, they'd be caught quickly. It wasn't the smart move, although it was definitely a tempting one. So she nodded her head. "We won't help him hurt Addie. That's not negotiable."

Donovan and Tess look back at her. They both nodded. "Agreed," Donovan said softly.

CHAPTER 9

ADDIE

THE SKY WAS STILL dark and bright with stars. But along the horizon, dawn had started to break its way through. Torr and I had quickly put together packs and taken off only a few minutes after I agreed to let him accompany me.

We ran almost nonstop that first day. We both knew we needed to get as far away as possible from Sterling Peak. But as night fell, the two of us were dragging. With the fight the night before, it had been thirty-six hours since we'd slept. So we took refuge in a small cave, unrolled our bedrolls, and both of us quickly fell asleep.

But I hadn't stayed asleep for long. Now I stared at the sky, as I been doing for the last few hours, trying to make sense of everything that had happened.

I had to have misunderstood what I saw with Graham and Donovan.

Marcus must have misunderstood or mistranslated the prophecy. After all, it had been around for decades. Why had no one realized the prophecy had been incorrectly translated before Marcus?

Lying here in the dark, it seemed so foolish to have taken off like that without at least being sure.

But Graham *had* hit Donovan. There was no mistaking that.

And that I couldn't explain. But there *had* to be an explanation. I looked over at where Torr slept soundly next to me. It was unusual for him to sleep so deeply, which showed just how tired he actually was. We had set a blistering pace. Torr wasn't used to running the way I was. And even for me, it was a lot.

But now I couldn't help but wonder if it was all for nothing. More than anything, I wanted to go back home and just make sure that leaving was the right decision.

I sighed, returning my eyes to the heavens. I really didn't know what the right call was here. Leaving Noel and Micah didn't feel right. But if Marcus was right, leaving was the best thing I could do for them.

At the same time, I knew they wouldn't see it that way, especially not Noel.

God, it was all such a mess. How had I ended up here?

It was almost as if angels and demons decided to work together to destroy the life I had started with the kids and Graham.

I flashed on the demon Abbadon's face. I knew him. I didn't know how, but I couldn't deny it. His was the first face that sparked any kind of recognition. But how? And what did that mean? However I knew him, it couldn't be good. Nothing that came from a demon could be good.

The thought brought me up short. But what if *I* came from a demon? The whole day I'd tried to keep Marcus's words from my mind. I focused on Graham and the archangel, but I'd stayed away from the thoughts of who my father actually was.

I had to admit, before all of this, I hadn't given much thought to my father. I thought maybe I had a mother out there somewhere who might be looking for me. And maybe a brother or sister. But I'd never really considered a father in any concrete way. And I didn't know what to think about Lucifer being that person.

Even the idea of it made me rebel. Lucifer was the ruler of Hell. How could *he* be my father? It didn't seem possible.

As far as I could remember, Lucifer had never even made an appearance during the Angel War. It was only his demons. And while Michael I had recognized on sight, there were no similar portraits of Lucifer. Nobody knew what he looked like.

Of course, I hadn't exactly had time to do an in-depth study of the Angel War. Although now it seemed like something that I was going to have to do, though I had no idea when or how I'd manage that.

Which brought me back to Graham and the reason I was lying on the hard ground staring up at dawn breaking along the horizon rather than back in Sterling Peak in a comfortable bed. Marcus must have been mistaken. I must have been mistaken. That was the only logical answer. Graham couldn't hurt me. It wasn't—

Movement along the tree line caused me to sit up quickly. I narrowed my eyes. Three shadows moved amongst the trees. Quietly, I reached over and touched Torr's shoulder.

His eyes flew open. I quickly held a finger to my lips. He nodded his understanding as he sat up and then got into a crouch. I pointed to the trees below.

I pulled the hood over my head and leaned back against the rock face while a shimmer rolled over Torr. The cloak was almost the same color as the rocks behind me. If I kept my head averted, they wouldn't even realize I was here. I watched them from the corner of my eye, my head to the side.

The men's voices carried through the quiet air.

"This is ridiculous."

"Do you want to go back and tell him that? Because I don't. I've never seen the commander look so angry."

"I mean, I know I don't know him as well as you guys do but he seemed ... different."

"Maybe it was the demon horde. Or the archangel Michael's visit. Either of those would change a person."

Three men stepped into view, leading their horses. Even in the dim light, I recognized the uniform of a Seraph Force Ranger.

"I suppose. But, man, I wouldn't like to be Addison Baker when he catches up with her."

"Yeah ..." The guard drawled out his word.

"What?"

"You didn't see her. According to Major Laura, Addison Baker was in the thick of it. She held the horde off single-handedly. And I saw her fly over with those wings. I don't know why he's after her, but it doesn't feel right."

"Well, it might not feel right, but that's what's happening. And we need to find her and bring her back whatever means necessary. You understand that, right, Ranger?"

The Ranger grunted. "I'll do my duty. Even if I don't like it."

The men moved into the trees, barely having even glanced up at the rock face. Torr and I sat silently, neither of us speaking until a full five minutes had passed.

"They were on horseback. That's how they were able to catch up to us so quickly," I said softly.

"Addie." Torr's eyes held a world of compassion.

But I shook my head, standing up. The guards' words had confirmed my fears. More than that, they broke my heart. But we didn't have time for that. I packed up my bedroll. "We need to get moving. We need to go faster."

Torr rolled up his bedroll as well and attached it to his pack. He slung it over his shoulders, cinching the straps. "Then we'll go faster."

I looked into his eyes and read the commitment there. I was grateful he was here, selfish as it was to let him to come along.

But now all I could think about was the fact that I hadn't been mistaken. Graham really was after me.

The morning was starting to warm, and yet a deep chill settled in my chest. Grabbing my pack, I started down the cliff face. "Let's get going."

CHAPTER 10

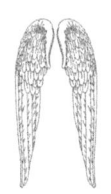

GRAHAM

Graham's head felt like a mariachi band was trying to pound its way out of his skull. Groaning, he rolled onto his back, and stared at the sunlight that streamed in through the edges of his drapes on the far side of the room. Had he gotten drunk? A large black empty space was all that he could pull up in his mind.

He couldn't remember drinking anything at all. Actually, he couldn't remember anything that would cause him to feel like this.

The demon horde and the fight that followed he could remember clearly. He pictured Addie in the middle of them, looking like a beautiful vision of death. Then he and Donovan had joined her. They'd split up, but he'd made it back to the bridge. Had she flown him?

Yeah, she had, and then she'd gone back for some reason. Torr? Had she gone looking for Torr? He struggled, but he couldn't remember seeing her after that.

At least, he didn't think he had. He vaguely remembered returning home. His shoulder had been dislocated. The doctor had insisted on setting it. Had the doctor snuck something into his drink? That wouldn't be like her, especially with the whole city in an uproar. She'd have let him tough it out. But why then couldn't he remember anything?

His shoulder. He'd rolled over in bed already, but there'd been no pain. Had he rolled on the other side? Shifting his shoulder, he tensed for the pain.

But there was none. He rolled it again, but there wasn't so much as a twinge of discomfort. What on earth was going on?

The door to his room flung open so hard it slammed against the wall. Franklin stormed in, muttering to himself as he walked over to the windows and yanked back the drapes. Sunlight glared into the room.

Graham winced, closing his eyes against the brightness. "What time is it?"

"Oh, is the master deigning to speak with the help?"

Graham frowned, sitting up slowly. Franklin continued around the room, picking up clothes and putting them down again, still muttering to himself. His face was tight, his whole body rigid. He was well and truly mad about something.

"What's wrong?"

"What's wrong? You're actually asking me what's wrong? Well, that's rich."

Graham stared at Franklin, the man who'd been more of a father to him than his actual father had ever been. "Are you mad at me?"

"Am I—" He cut off his sentence, rolling his fists as he tightened his lips, seeming to try to get his anger under control. Without a word, he studied Graham from head to toe. His inspection did nothing to curtail his anger. His words snapped out through gritted teeth. "Your behavior has not been even *close* to acceptable."

Graham's mind struggled through the molasses of his memories. But he had nothing but a big blank space after coming back to the estate. "Franklin, I don't know what you're talking about.

Did the doctor do something different to my arm? It doesn't hurt at all. And what about the horde? What was the damage? Did Addie come back?"

Franklin's angry look was replaced by one of confusion. He spoke slowly. "What's the last thing you remember?"

Graham shook his head. Pain lanced through his forehead, making him immediately stop the motion. He frowned, concentrating. "Addie at the bridge. She went to go look for Torr. I got my arm checked out. I gave in because I knew until I got my arm set, I wouldn't be any use in a fight. And the horde was about to arrive."

"The horde turned back."

Graham frowned. "Why? Was it the bridge? It worked? They couldn't cross it?"

That had been the original intent behind the bridge, although Graham had always thought it was a stopgap. The demons would find a way.

"Do you remember the archangel?"

Graham's head jolted up, and he winced. He really needed to stop moving so quickly. "The archangel? What are you talking about?"

Franklin ran a hand through his hair. "You don't remember the archangel Michael appearing and dropping down right in your backyard?"

Graham's eyes widened as he studied Franklin. His anger was out of character for him, and now this crazy story? "Are you okay? Did you hit your head or something?"

Franklin shook his head, his eyes troubled. "Something's wrong here. Stay here. I'll be right back." Without another word, Franklin hastened from the room.

Graham watched the open doorway, trying to wrap his head around what Franklin had said. The archangel Michael had appeared? That was impossible. Graham certainly wouldn't forget something that momentous.

He had to admit, though, that his memory had a gaping hole in it from the time he got back to the estate until waking up just now. But surely he wouldn't have forgotten an archangel, right?

Graham shifted to the edge of the bed, dropping his legs over the side. He rolled his shoulder again. No pain. That made no sense. He had definitely dislocated it. Flying with Addie had been near agony; he remembered that. But they'd had no choice.

Yet there wasn't so much as a twinge of discomfort now. Fear began to crawl over him. *How long was I asleep?* Maybe the battle had been days ago, weeks ago if his shoulder was any indication. Had he been hurt worse that he thought?

He stood up and walked to the bathroom and splashed water on his face. Staring at his reflection, he saw not a single cut, abrasion, or bruise. There wasn't a scratch on him.

The battle must've been days ago. *Have I been sick?*

But that didn't explain Franklin's mood. If he'd been that sick, Franklin would have been happy Graham was awake, not mad. Surely if he was delirious with fever, Franklin wouldn't hold whatever ridiculous ramblings had come out of his mouth against him.

After leaving the bathroom, Graham pulled on a T-shirt from the wardrobe. He really wanted a shower, but he needed answers first. He'd just turned around, planning on tracking down Donovan to see what was going on, when Franklin reappeared in the doorway, Donovan and Marcus right behind him. Both of them appeared just as angry as Franklin had been.

Graham's steps faltered as he looked between them. "Hi, guys. Uh, what's going on?"

Marcus stepped forward, but Donovan held out a hand. "You don't go near him."

Donovan doesn't trust me. It was like a punch to the gut. If Franklin was like his father, Donovan was most definitely his brother. "What's going on, guys? Why are you acting like I'm the enemy?"

Donovan glared at him. "Because you've demonstrated that maybe you are."

The words slapped Graham in the face. He took as step back, shock rolling through him. "What?"

Donovan continued. "I never thought you were like your brother. But for the last two days, you've shown you could be even worse."

The words cut right through Graham. Donovan knew Graham was nothing like his brother. He knew that. Why would he say such a thing?

Graham took another step back and sat down on the chair by the window, careful to keep himself on the other side of the room. And he hated that he was doing it so that his friends felt comfortable. "I don't understand what you guys are talking about. Start at the beginning. The last thing I remember, I was coming back to the house get my shoulder set. Then the next thing I know, I'm waking up here, only my shoulder's fine and everybody's mad at me. How long ago was the demon attack? And where's Addie? Did she find Torr?"

Donovan's anger, which seemed to soften as Graham spoke, returned at full force with the mention of Addie's name. He crossed his arms over his chest. "So that's your game now? Pretend you're our friend so we'll tell you where she is? No chance."

Graham wanted to scream, he was so frustrated. He gritted his teeth. "I don't know what you're talking about. How long ago was the attack?"

"It was two nights ago," Franklin said.

Graham stared at them, trying to make sense of that timeline. He spoke slowly. "That's not possible. My shoulder was dislocated. It's not now. There's no way it could heal in a matter of days."

"It was healed in a matter of seconds," Marcus said, studying him intently.

Graham's mouth fell open. "What?"

"Oh, for God's sake." Franklin stepped forward. "The archangel Michael healed you when he arrived. You met him on the back lawn. Then a bright light engulfed you, and when it was gone, you were changed. You were someone else. Donovan's right: you were worse than your brother."

A feeling of dread fell over Graham. "What did I do?"

"Nothing, nobody was hurt," Marcus said quickly.

"Except for Micah," Donovan spat.

Graham's mouth fell open. "Micah? I hurt Micah? On purpose?"

"You were trying to get him tell you where Addie had gone. You threatened Micah with a knife to get him and Noel to talk."

"Where Addie had gone? She's not here?" Graham asked.

Donovan's glare increased, his anger clearly getting more intense. Okay, apparently Addie was completely off-limits right now.

Graham held up his hands. "Okay, look, I feel like I'm only getting bits and pieces of this story. Can you please start at the beginning? Because I honestly have zero memories from just after Addie brought me back."

"We need to tell him," Franklin said.

Donovan shook his head. "No."

Franklin let out an exasperated sigh. "We can't help him find Addie. We've no idea where she is. If he's trying to trick us to get information, then it's a pretty lousy trick."

Franklin and Marcus waited, watching Donovan for his permission. Finally, Donovan nodded. Marcus started to step forward, but once again, Donovan held out his hand. "Tell him from here."

Marcus took a breath. "What Franklin said is true. Two nights ago, the archangel Michael descended onto your back lawn. You spoke with him."

Graham gaped at Marcus. "I don't remember that. How can I not remember that?"

"There's more," Donovan said.

Graham listened in growing horror as Marcus recounted Graham's search for Addie. How he'd sent scouts out, telling them to use whatever means were necessary to bring her back. Donovan took over the telling about how he had terrified and threatened Noel and Micah and punched Donovan.

Then Marcus took over again, explaining how Graham had shown no interest in the refugees from Blue Forks, his entire focus on developing a strategy to track Addie down.

Marcus's recounting was quiet and concise. But each word felt like a dagger to Graham's chest. He didn't say a word until Marcus fell silent. "I don't remember any of that." He looked up. "Is Micah all right?"

"No thanks to you," Donovan said, although the bite in his words was reduced. "You have them under guard in your house right now."

Well, at least he knew what to say to that. "Release them immediately. I still don't get why I did all that."

"It's because you were determined to find Addie," Donovan said.

Graham could understand that motivation. He could understand needing to know that Addie was okay after everything. But why would he threaten Noel and Micah? They would want to know Addie was okay just as much as he would. "This doesn't make any sense."

Marcus studied Graham. "How do you feel about Addie now?"

Graham swallowed. "I care about her. I'm worried about her. She hasn't come back since she went looking for Torr. She could be hurt or—"

"She did come back," Marcus said quietly. "She came to your house. She was here when the angel arrived."

Graham frowned. "Why would I be looking for her if she was already here?"

"Because I told her to run," Marcus said. "I told her to get as far away from you as she possibly could."

Some of Graham's concern shifted to anger. "Why would you do that?"

"Because I knew if you saw Addie, you would try to kill her. And because she cares about you, she wouldn't defend herself as strongly as she needed to. And you would have succeeded."

Shock rippled through Graham. "I would never hurt Addie."

Marcus sighed. "I know you mean that, but I'm not sure it's entirely your choice anymore."

CHAPTER 11

NOEL

Noel stood quietly by the window. They were at Graham's estate. Before the archangel, it had started to feel almost like home, or at least not like enemy territory. Mary always seemed to have food ready for them, and she and Franklin were always looking out for them. Donovan, Tess, and Laura would always stop by, and of course, Marcus and Graham. And then, of course, Addie had always been with them.

Now Graham's estate felt like a prison.

It had been two days since the archangel had changed everything, but it felt so much longer. Noel supposed if she'd slept a little more at night, time might move faster. But she felt like she'd taken little more than catnaps over the last two days.

And even for those few moments when she managed to drift off, it wasn't a deep sleep. Because even in sleep, she was on edge, ready to wake at a moment's notice if Micah had another nightmare, if a demon attack occurred, or worse, if Graham returned.

But she'd barely seen him for the last two days, and for that, she was grateful.

They hadn't been restricted to their room, which had surprised her. But every time they stepped outside the door, they had two shadows. The Rangers who followed them never said anything. They never tried to stop them from going anywhere. They were just this constant oppressive presence.

They even looked a little guilty, depending on who the guards were. But Noel supposed they had nothing to feel guilty for. It was Graham who should feel guilty, but he didn't seem to suffer from such emotions right now.

Rage rolled through Noel as she pictured Graham with his knife pressed against Micah's neck, his eyes cold.

She never would've thought that Graham was capable of that kind of cruelty, but now her eyes were open. Now she knew who the real Graham was.

On the walk back to the estate, Donovan and Tess seemed to be in shock, trying to figure out why Graham would behave that way. But Noel had blocked them out, her attention completely on Micah. He'd been shaking almost the whole way, and for the last two nights he'd been wracked by nightmares. Each night, he'd only fallen off to sleep close to daybreak.

Noel knew she should probably get some sleep too, but she just couldn't close her eyes. She needed to figure out a way to get Micah to safety.

She had met Micah in the Young Sparrow Orphanage. The place had gotten its name from the street outside, which had once upon a time been Sparrow Lane. It had been a plain two-story building with long open rooms. No one knew what the building had been before.

There'd been a rumor that it had once been an insane asylum and that the bodies of the former patients had been buried in the small yard out back. Noel didn't believe that, at least not during the day. But at night, it was hard not to imagine desiccated corpses pushing themselves from their unsanctified graves.

She and Micah had spent nearly three years in that hellhole.

When he'd first arrived, he'd been so small that he'd been mistaken for a four-year-old, even though he was six. The other kids had picked on him. And in the orphanage, Noel had taken it upon herself to be his protector.

The staff had been more interested in what was in the bottom of their cups than interceding. Sometimes they even encouraged the violence. There was one supervisor, Thad, who liked to pit the kids against one another. He called it his own little Thunderdome. He said he was preparing them for the cold, dark world they would face when they finally left the orphanage.

When the demons attacked, Thad had been one of the first killed. Not because he ran forward to defend them. No, good old Thad sprinted out of the common room as soon as the demons busted down the front door. All the kids tried to rush after him, but he locked the door behind him. The kids had gone out through the windows, those who survived. As Noel boosted Micah out the window, she'd heard Thad's cry, high and filled with pain.

And she hadn't felt an inkling of compassion. He deserved all that pain and much more.

After escaping the orphanage, she and Micah had run. They'd hidden in the woods for a few days, but hunger sent them back to civilization.

They stayed away from Nichols Inlet, not sure if anyone was looking for them. Because no matter what happened, both of them agreed they would not go back to a state-run orphanage. If they had to, they'd live in the woods.

For the next year, they lived out there almost full time. The good thing about the woods was that they never saw a demon out there. The bad thing was the lack of food and the cold. There were a few fruit trees and bushes, but it wasn't enough.

So every few days, Noel would sneak into Blue Forks and steal her and Micah some food. She wasn't proud of it, but she *was* proud of the fact that she'd kept herself and Micah alive. But even so, it had been a terrifying time. Their bellies had always felt hollow, and they had no safe ground.

Then they'd met Addie.

The three of them had become a family. Noel could honestly say that the last two years had been the best of her life. She had people she could trust. People who actually loved her. But now Addie was gone, and Micah was terrified again.

And Noel was so damn mad at the world she could barely see straight.

Donovan and Tess promised that one of them or Laura would always be in Graham's home. They would never leave them alone.

Noel appreciated the words, but she wasn't planning on trusting them. They were under Graham's command. She knew that if push came to shove, they would probably side with him. Micah and Addie were the only ones she truly trusted.

And she had no idea where Addie was.

Or Torr. She had a feeling he'd gone with Addie. She wasn't sure how to feel about that. On the one hand, she felt better at the idea of Addie not being alone. But on the other hand, she couldn't help but be hurt that Addie hadn't taken her and Micah too.

But she didn't dwell too much on the hurt. She'd learned long ago that was useless. What was useful was information.

She needed to know what was going on. That was the first step in getting her family back together. That was the first step in keeping Micah safe.

Micah was still in a deep sleep, lying on his stomach, his arms flung wide. She hated the idea of leaving him alone, and she prayed he didn't wake up anytime soon, but she really did need to get some answers. And if anyone had them, it would be Marcus. She hadn't seen him since they arrived. But she and Micah hadn't exactly been wandering around much.

But she knew Marcus was here. Franklin had told her when he'd looked in on them a little while ago.

She walked over to the bed and arranged the covers, tucking

them around Micah a little tighter. She leaned down and kissed him on the forehead. "I'll be right back," she whispered.

Quickly walking across the room, she stopped at the door and glanced back at him. She'd only be down the hall. It would be all right.

They had been placed back in the room that she and Micah had been given after the attack down in Blue Forks. She'd half expected them to be placed in some sort of dungeon. But at least if they were going to be stuck, it was here rather than in some damp, dark cell. The door to the other room, where Torr had stayed, had been locked.

Noel's heart sank, once again seesawing between hoping he was with Addie and hoping he was trying to get back to them.

She liked Torr. And knowing he had been around them, looking out for them, made it easy to overlook the green skin and the beginning of horns. Because in his heart, before Addie, Torr had been just like her and Micah: lost. She prayed that he stayed away, stayed hidden. She didn't know what Graham would do to him in his current state. Tears pressed against her eyes. God, things were so messed up.

Noel eased open the door. Donovan stood right outside. His head jolted up as she stepped into the hall. He blinked a few times and wiped his eyes. "Hey, Noel, have you gotten any sleep?"

Noel shook her head. "No, not yet. I need some answers now that we're not under house arrest."

Donovan had stopped in earlier to tell them that Graham had removed that restriction. Noel's first instinct was to grab Micah and run.

But that would have been foolish; she didn't know where they could go.

So with or without the guards' presence, she still felt the same: trapped.

Donovan stared into her eyes and nodded. "Hold on one

second." He walked to the end of the hall and then let out a whistle.

Tess jogged up the stairs just a few seconds later. "What's going on?"

"I'm going to take Noel to speak with Marcus. Micah's still inside. Will you take the door?"

Tess met Noel's gaze. Noel looked away, embarrassed by her tears. But Tess didn't say anything about it. She merely stepped in front of the door. "I got it."

Noel felt a little better. It did seem like the two of them were keeping an eye on them, but she still couldn't be sure if they were keeping an eye on them for Graham or from Graham.

Donovan returned with a nod. "Marcus is up. So let's go get you some answers."

CHAPTER 12

GRAHAM

GRAHAM SAT on the side patio of his home. There was a slight breeze, but it was still warm. It felt like there was tension in the air in Sterling Peak, or maybe everyone else was fine and it was just him.

This was the spot where Marcus had told Addie that if Graham saw her, he would kill her.

Marcus had explained about the prophecy. The archangel had done something to him, had somehow removed his free will. Graham felt angry at the mere idea of being used as a puppet. At the same time, he struggled to accept that it was even possible. Surely he wouldn't have actually harmed Addie, would he?

But he'd seen the distrust on the faces of Franklin, Marcus, and Donovan. And he'd seen the fear on the faces of Noel and Micah. He didn't doubt that he'd done what they said. At the same time, he recoiled from the idea of it. Everything in him screamed that there was no way he would harm a child. And yet...

He leaned over, dropping his head into his hands. He had finally found a rhythm as the leader of the Seraph Force. He'd figured out, for the most part, how to balance the needs of the elite and doing the right thing. And he'd found Addie.

But now he didn't trust himself. Why was this happening?

The clearing of a throat caused him to raise his head.

Franklin sat down next to him. Guilt and shame rushed through him. Donovan had explained how he'd ordered Franklin and Mary about yesterday like the king of the castle. "I'm so sorry, Franklin. You don't deserve to be treated the way I treated you. You know how much you and Mary mean to me. I just—"

Franklin put up a hand. "I don't know what happened with the archangel. But he did change you. The man I saw wasn't you. And Donovan was right, you were much like your brother, God forgive me for saying it. And he was an evil man."

Graham nodded. His brother had harbored a black heart. Graham had been on the receiving end of it for all of his childhood. "I don't understand how I could have done any of that."

Franklin sighed, shifting in his seat and crossing his feet at the ankles. "Decades have passed since the Angel War, since the angels sent the demons back into Hell. And the stories we've told each other since then have taken on a similar theme: the heroic angels and the villainous demons. Young Torr has made me question some of the demon beliefs, but still I clung to the image of the angels as the heroes.

"When we tell the stories, we speak of the angels' eventual victory. But that's not all there was in the war. My grandmother was just a child during it. Her entire village was nearly wiped out when the angels destroyed a dam to wash away the demons. Under the torrent of water, countless humans lost their lives too. There are thousands of stories like that. Demons and humans dying together. And I have to wonder if maybe there wasn't a better way.

"But the angels didn't care what got in their way. Everything was an obstacle to their main objective: destroying the demons.

Humans who stepped in that path were destroyed as well. No one was an impediment to the angels' primary mission.

"The more I think about your behavior yesterday, the more I see how much you had in common with those angel warriors. You were without compassion, without emotion. All you saw was your goal. And your goal was to find Addie."

Graham had heard the stories about the wars, and just like everyone else, he'd glossed over the atrocities committed by the angels while focusing on the atrocities of the demons. After all these years, it was easy to discount nameless, faceless victims. But now the victims had faces. And they were the faces of Noel and Micah. "I don't like that. I don't like any of it."

"I know, but for the last two days, you have been single-minded in your focus. Finding Addie was all that you were concerned with. No other factors came into play."

"Do you think I could have killed someone?"

Franklin didn't hesitate. "You could have. You forget when they tell stories that the angels were jealous. And that jealousy has made them even more dangerous to all of us."

Graham knew that was true. That the angels were envious of humans' free will. And he couldn't help but wonder if that envy had led them to be careless with human lives. "I want to be the one in control of my life. I should be able to choose who I love and what I will fight for."

"The angel removed your ability to choose. He made you less human. He made you—"

"Like them," Graham said softly.

Franklin nodded.

Graham stared off into the distance, beyond the mountains that protected Sterling Peak's back. Normally, the sight of them filled him with wonder at such beauty. But today he felt cold, cold and filled with fear at what he could have done and what he could still do, because in the corner of his mind, ever since he'd woken up, he'd felt this presence lurking, growing larger. "I want to say that I will fight this. That I won't let the angels use me for their own ends. But I can't guarantee that. So I need you to promise me something."

"What?"

"This isn't over. I don't why I have this short reprieve, but it isn't over. I will get lost again. You need to keep people out of my way. I need you to understand: It's not that I agree with the archangel's goal, but I can't let other people get hurt. And when I speak to you—"

"Neither Mary nor I will believe you. We know now it's not you. I will do everything in my power to make sure that your ability to harm anyone is neutralized."

Graham felt a small sliver of relief at his words. He wasn't sure what Franklin could actually do, but the idea that he understood and that he would take pains to protect those around him made Graham feel much better.

Graham stood up, staring out over the yard. "It's still so hard to believe."

Franklin stood and joined him. "Having seen it with my own eyes, I still have trouble believing it." He placed his hand on Graham's shoulder. "I know who you are. And if anyone can fight this, it's you. Just hold on to who you are. It will see you through."

Graham didn't know what to say. Franklin's faith in him was humbling. He prayed to God that it was well-placed.

CHAPTER 13

NOEL

N oel followed Donovan down the hall. He knocked softly on Marcus's door.

"Come in," came the muffled reply.

Marcus looked up from behind his desk as Donovan opened the door. He sprang to his feet as soon as he saw Noel. "Noel. How are you? Are you all right? I'm sorry. I'm so sorry—"

"I know, Marcus. I know."

And she did. She just wished it was all different.

But that wish was one she had been making her whole life. And one that she knew would never come true. The deck was most royally stacked against her. She'd accepted that a long time ago.

The concern on Marcus's face cut through some of Noel's defenses. She took a stuttering breath. "I'm fine. Did you hear what—"

Marcus nodded his head. "Yes. I heard what Graham did. And I've seen ..." He paused. "Graham."

"What's going on, Marcus?" Noel asked. "I've never seen Graham behave this way. This isn't him."

Marcus waved them over to the couch. Noel sank into the corner of it, her whole body suddenly feeling tired and nervous. She wanted answers, but at the same time, she was scared of what they would be. What if this was who Graham actually was? What if they had all been fooled?

"I've spent the last few days spending every spare minute going through every relevant book—"

Noel cut in. "Books? Graham's transformation into his own evil twin hasn't been your focus?"

Marcus sighed wearily. "I'm afraid not. Graham has had me researching a ... different topic."

"Addie," Noel said softly.

"Yes. I've been locked away in the Academy's library. But I'll get to that in a minute." Marcus sat next to her. "How much do you know about what happened at the estate before Graham went down to the bridge?"

Noel shrugged. "Not much. Someone mentioned something about an archangel."

"Yes. The archangel Michael descended from the sky. He landed in Graham's yard. Graham went out to meet him. He healed Graham's shoulder. And then he placed his hands on Graham's face, and he removed his free will."

Noel stared at Marcus for a few moments. "His free will? What does that mean?"

Marcus shifted in his seat as if trying to get more comfortable. And for the first time, Noel noticed the bags under his eyes. He looked completely exhausted.

"When angels were created, they were expressly made to fulfill God's orders. They cannot make decisions for themselves. They must do what they have been ordered to do. Humans are not like that. We can choose what we do, where we go, who we spend time with."

"Doesn't feel like that," Noel said, thinking about how separated society was. The Angel Blessed might have those luxuries, but the Demon Cursed certainly didn't.

Marcus gave her a small smile. "I know it feels like that at times. But even with society's rules and expectations, we still have choices. We don't have to choose what everyone wants us to do. We have to face the consequences of those choices, of course, but we could actually *make* the choice. For the angels, there is no choice. They must follow the orders they are given."

"And that's what Graham is like now?" Noel asked.

Marcus nodded. "I was going through the books, trying to see if this had ever happened before. There were some documented cases during the Angel War of other humans having their free will removed. For those humans, they were needed by the angels for particular missions. And so their free will was taken so that they could complete those missions without any human emotions getting in the way."

"So that wasn't really Graham," Donovan said softly.

Marcus looked over at him. "Make no mistake, when an angel removes a human's free will, they cannot fight it. They must do what they have been commanded. It is not Graham in the sense that if he had his free will, he would not make those choices. But without that ability to choose, he will do what the angel has ordered of him. When you see him, you cannot think of him as your friend. Because without his free will, he is not. He will be as single-minded as the angels were during the war. The only thing that he will focus on is his duty. And his duty right now is to find Addie."

Noel cut in. "I don't understand that. Why does he want to find Addie? Why does he want to hurt her?"

"It all goes back to an ancient prophecy. About the final fight between the forces of good and evil."

Noel had to rein in her frustration. "But what does Addie have to do with that? I mean, are the angels now on the side of evil?"

Marcus's voice softened. "No, the angels aren't on the side of evil."

Noel stared at him, trying to figure out what he was attempting to say. And then it hit her. She sat up straight, glaring at Marcus. "You can't think *Addie* is on the side of evil? That's insane."

Marcus held up his hands. "I don't think Addie is evil. But you don't know everything about her—"

Noel cut him off. "I know her better than any of you. She saved us. She's saved countless people. She saved all of Blue Forks. And you're trying to tell me she's evil?"

Marcus put up his hands in a pleading gesture. "I don't think it's that simple. There's a prophecy. She's destined to fight the powers of good."

"Why?" Noel asked. "Why Addie? She's a good person. All she's ever *done* is help people."

"I know. The problem is not who Addie is, exactly. The problem is who her father is."

The answer caught Noel up short. "Who her father is? Addie doesn't know who her father is." Noel stared at Marcus's face. "But you do. Her father's an archangel, isn't he?"

"Yes. He's an archangel," Marcus said. "At one point, one of the most favored."

There was something about Marcus's tone. Something that made her nervous. "Who? Who's Addie's father?"

Marcus didn't answer right away. Noel worried for a moment that he wasn't going to answer at all. But finally he spoke. "Lucifer. Lucifer is Addie's father."

Noel's jaw dropped open. She flicked a glance to check Donovan's reaction, but he was completely unfazed. He already knew. She turned her attention back to Marcus. "No. That's not possible."

"I assure you that it is. I've been scouring the books for days. It was when I saw her wings that it all came together. She's the child of fire, and her father is Lucifer."

Noel stood up. "I won't listen to this. You don't know Addie. She's a good person. She wouldn't—"

Donovan stood up as well blocking her exit. "He's not saying this to hurt her or you. He's just trying to understand. We're all caught in something bigger than ourselves. I don't know what it means that Addie is the daughter of Lucifer. What I do know is that my best friend, who I've known since we were kids, has turned into someone I don't even recognize. And I know you love Addie, but after seeing Graham transform, I don't think that anything is off the table right now. Addie doesn't remember her life before two years ago, right?"

Reluctantly, Noel nodded.

Donovan's voice was soft, full of understanding, but it didn't change the fact that Noel hated every word that came out of his mouth. "What happens when she does remember? None of us know who she was before that point. And maybe when she gets those memories back, it will change everything, just like the archangel changed Graham."

Noel wrapped her arms around herself, suddenly feeling cold. "That won't happen. You don't know her." But Noel could hear the doubt in her own voice, and she hated herself for it.

Because Donovan was right. They didn't know anything about Addie before two years ago. And while everything in her screamed that Addie was good, she couldn't deny that she'd seen the change in Graham. She couldn't deny that the people who knew him best, the people who had known him his entire life, were completely shocked at the transformation.

And it was true. She had only known Addie for two years. Could she really say for sure that Addie wouldn't change if she remembered her life before?

Noel sank back onto the couch, suddenly feeling like the world was a lot colder than it had been just moments ago.

CHAPTER 14

GRAHAM

Franklin had gone back inside while Graham stayed outside, staring up at the sky. Graham knew he was remaining outside because he didn't trust himself to be around other people, especially not Noel or Micah. He didn't want to add any more fear to the current situation.

At the same time, he didn't know how to keep something like that from happening again. He could feel this strange presence lurking at the edges of his consciousness. He wanted to believe that whatever had happened to him was now over. That it had been a one-time thing, and now he could return to life as usual. But he felt in his gut that it was only a matter of time.

The door opened behind him. He glanced over his shoulder as Donovan stepped through. Donovan's body was stiff, even his voice, as he spoke. "Franklin said you wanted to see me."

"Yes." Graham nodded as he stood. Then he just stood staring at his friend.

Donovan stared back at him as if he didn't trust him.

And Graham knew that he had every right to feel that way. But it didn't change the fact that that it hurt. "I'm sorry. Everything that happened ... I'm just sorry for all of it. But I know it's going to happen again."

Donovan's eyes narrowed as he studied Graham. And Graham knew he was looking to see if he had already changed. Graham didn't know how to explain it, but he could feel the creep from inside coming over his mind. He knew it was only a matter of time before he was no longer in control again.

"I need you to promise me something."

Donovan gave him a stiff nod. "What is it?"

"Do not let me hurt anyone. Do whatever you need to do, but do not let me hurt anyone. I don't know what the angel has planned. But I won't let someone get hurt at my hands." He paused, thinking of Micah. "Not again. You do whatever it takes to make sure that people are safe from me. Do you understand?"

Donovan gave him a nod, his face softening. "Graham—"

The darkness that had been creeping at the edges of Graham's mind slammed shut over it. Unlike before, when he had no memory, now he felt as if he was trapped in part of his brain while left looking out. "What is the report from the scouts?" he demanded.

Donovan stared at him for a long moment before his face became an icy mask. "Nothing from them yet."

"Find them. Send out another group. Send ten more. Track down the original scouts, get whatever information they have and relay it back. Send them with the hawks. I want to know where Addison Baker is."

Donovan stiffened as he watched Graham through narrowed eyes.

Inside his own mind, Graham beat his hands against the invisible wall holding him back. *It's not me, Donovan. Know it's not me.* But those weren't the words that came out of his mouth. "Is that going to be a problem?"

Donovan shook his head. "No, it's not a problem."

Then Donovan inclined his head, turned on his heel, and left.

Graham watched Donovan leave. Donovan was the second-in-command of the Seraph Force. If anything should happen to Graham, Donovan would immediately take over.

But that wasn't going to work. He needed to find Addison Baker. And Donovan would not do what was necessary to make that happen.

Graham strode into the house. He caught sight of one of the Rangers. He called him over. "Miles."

The Ranger who was crossing the foyer stopped and turned toward him. "Yes, Commander?"

"Send word to Major D'Angelo. I need to speak with him immediately."

CHAPTER 15

NOEL

D<small>ONOVAN HAD BEEN CALLED AWAY</small>, so Noel grilled Marcus herself. She didn't like the answers he gave her, but she also didn't think he was being untruthful.

And Noel really didn't know what to do with those answers. Micah was still asleep when Noel slipped back into the room. Instead of joining him on the bed, she went and grabbed a blanket and curled up on the chair over by the fireplace.

Addie was the daughter of Lucifer. Noel couldn't wrap her mind around it. Lucifer was the Devil, the incarnation of evil. How could Addie be his child?

At the orphanage, they had been taught about the Angel War, of course, and they had also been taught about the fallen angels. Lucifer hadn't been seen during the Angel War, although the demons were believed to be his minions.

Lucifer, at one time, had been one of the most favored of the angels in Heaven. In the stories, he'd become jealous of humanity, of their free will, and he had been cast out of Heaven. The angels who sided with him—which, according to the old tales, was one third of all of the angels—had been cast out with him, and they were the first of the demons.

Noel pulled her knees up to her chin, wrapping her arms around them as she stared at Micah sleeping on the bed. And now Addie was supposed to be his daughter.

Was that even possible? Nothing about Addie screamed evil. She seemed to go out of her way to help people. So how was it possible that she was the daughter of the most evil angel?

Although when she thought about it, were the things Lucifer did really so evil? He wanted to make decisions for himself. That seemed rather normal, not exactly evil.

She knew that in the military, soldiers were expected to follow the chain of command. It seemed like for the angels, that extended well beyond just their duties. In fact, it seemed like all they had was duty. Duty and no life. She could imagine that watching humans going through their lives and enjoying themselves would be tough, knowing that they were not allowed the same luxuries.

But even as she tried to twist Lucifer and the fallen angels' actions into something good, she knew that the demons themselves were not good. They had wreaked havoc upon the planet. They were cruel. They were violent. They were killers.

Well, except for Torr, of course. He wasn't like them. She didn't know how to explain him, but all the others who she'd met or heard of were decidedly not like him.

At the same time, the idea that Addie was somehow demon related just did not sit well with her.

And why was she taking Marcus's and Donovan's word for it anyway? Marcus and Donovan didn't know Addie the way she and Micah did. She'd only met Marcus and Donovan a short while ago. Addie had been the one who had fought for her and Micah. She was the one who had taken care of them. She was the one who had looked out for them, who had gone hungry so that they could eat.

She didn't think Marcus was trying to be unkind in his explanation, but there had to be something he was missing. He was getting his information from old dusty books. Addie was neither old nor dusty. And those books didn't apply to her.

Noel nodded her head. She would find Addie. And then together, they would figure out what was going on. It was the only way forward.

Decision made, she felt the exhaustion fall over her. She needed to sleep. In her current state, she wouldn't be able to walk anywhere. So she would sleep, and when she woke up, she and Micah would find Addie, and they would learn what was going on. Then they would come up with a plan together.

CHAPTER 16

ADDIE

It had been a long couple of days. I wiped at my face as if somehow I could remove some of my exhaustion and instill some energy. It didn't work. My limbs still felt as if they weighed an extra ten pounds each.

Torr and I hadn't stopped moving since we'd seen the Rangers. Torr could run almost as fast as I could, so during the day we ran. At night, when it was dark and there were no people or towns around, I would fly Torr. He would sleep during some of that time, but I stayed awake the whole time.

After seeing the scouts, we'd picked up our pace and went through more desolate country. Sleeping hadn't been much of an option. I'd caught an hour here or there at best. But now that lack of sleep was catching up with me. We'd headed a little more northeast, figuring going inland was probably better than staying along the coast. We hoped it would provide us with more places to hide.

There were a few small villages that we saw, but we'd made

sure to give them a wide berth so that there were no witnesses to our passing.

I still struggled to believe everything that had happened. At times I simply couldn't and wondered if maybe we should go back. I kept clinging to the notion that this was all just a horrible misunderstanding.

An image of Graham's face and the lack of emotion on it flashed through my mind, followed by the fear in Marcus's voice.

No, it wasn't a dream. It wasn't a misunderstanding. Graham and I were destined to fight to the death. And I knew in my heart that if it came down to it, I wouldn't be able to kill him. I just wouldn't.

Torr stumbled on the uneven ground. My hand shot out and grabbed hold of him before he could pitch forward. "You okay?"

"Yeah, I'm fine. Just a little …" He waved his hand without finishing the thought.

But I knew what he meant. He was just a little exhausted, just a little tired beyond reason.

"We should probably find a place to sleep for a few hours. We've been going nonstop. We need to rest."

Torr didn't argue with me. He simply nodded his head, which worried me even more. He must be really exhausted. "Yeah, I think that's a good idea."

It was getting toward the end of the night. I'd been too tired to fly carrying Torr, so we'd stayed on the ground. But we'd been lucky and hadn't run into any demons so far. I wasn't overly surprised by that. There was no sense in the demons sticking around in areas we'd been. They were completely unpopulated. It would make more sense for them to stay closer to the population centers.

"Look."

Torr pointed to the horizon, where the first rays of sunlight were just beginning to catch the night sky. I smiled at the sight of it and Torr's face. Torr loved the first lights of the day. Each morning he stopped for just a few seconds to watch it. And then, as we walked, I would catch his gaze constantly straying to the horizon.

"Addie?"

My head jerked up, my eyes flying open. I had just nearly fallen asleep standing up. I blinked my eyes a couple of times. "I'm good."

But I knew that wasn't true. We really needed to find a place to lie down for a little while. I wasn't going to be able to go much farther.

Pulling out my water flask, I took some sips hoping it would revive me a little. The water was lukewarm and running low. We'd need to find a water source as well.

We walked for another few minutes in silence. My feet dragged along the ground, leaving an obvious trail but I couldn't seem to pull them up higher. Ahead, I could make out the vague outline of the town that we'd seen from up on the hill. There'd been no movement in the town, no lights or fires. It seemed like it was deserted. As we got closer, there was still no movement, but because it was early, that didn't necessarily mean anything, so we went carefully.

We came over a rise and stared at the small city spread out in front of us. It looked abandoned, just like countless others we'd seen on our trip thus far.

I hadn't realized just how devastated the country had been after the Angel War. I figured that there were cities like Sterling Peak and Blue Forks spread all over the place. I knew that disease and famine had wiped out large portions of the population, but I hadn't really imagined what that would look like.

But now I knew. It looked like a wasteland. We'd traveled around cities that were now skeletons of their former selves. There were people in some of them, but only a couple dozen or so. And they were hard to look to at: emaciated frames, skin darkened by a lack of water, soap, or both.

The small town in front of us wasn't a big city, though. There were only about a dozen or so buildings on Main Street and another half dozen or so homes spread out beyond it. The tallest building was three stories tall and had peaked corners. I nodded toward it. "Let's check it out. We might be able to find a safe place to camp in there for the rest of the day."

Torr nodded, practically swaying on his feet. We were both in pretty rough shape. Ignoring the exhaustion pulling at me, I headed toward the town. Just a little more, and we could take a break.

Sadly, the distance was deceiving. It took us another thirty minutes before we crossed into the town limits. The only reason we knew that we had was because there was a metal sign that had fallen over on its side. Pitkin, established in 1882, population 416.

I looked around the town. Nothing moved. Apparently there hadn't been anyone around to update the town's population.

A shimmer rolled over Torr, and I knew he'd just blocked himself from anyone else's view. He stayed invisible whenever we were near any towns. The fact that he'd only done it right now indicated just how tired he was.

We moved to the side of what used to be a road but was now little more than cracked asphalt. The first two buildings we came to were almost completely collapsed. Two walls stood in one, and in the other a single wall balanced against a pile of rubble. It would be suicide to attempt to take shelter within them.

My energy was draining fast, so I picked up the pace. We checked the next few buildings, but my eyes kept drifting back to a large building at the end of the street. It was probably our best bet.

But as we approached it, I saw another building that offered a possibility. It was an old hardware store, the shelves completely cleared. Torr nodded toward it. "We can stay here."

I nodded, but once again the building at the end of the road kept pulling my attention. "Let's check out the rest of the town first. I don't want to get surprised by anyone."

We passed the large building. We'd search that last. But we were close enough to read the metal sign affixed to the side of the large wooden doors: PITKIN PUBLIC LIBRARY.

The brick building itself looked like it was in good shape. The windows were still intact.

My heart began to beat faster. A library. I'd never been in one. I'd never even seen one. There were none in Sterling Peak except up at the Academy, and I'd never been there. They sounded like heaven: rows and rows of books. Noel would be overjoyed.

The thought of Noel sent a stab of homesickness through me. God, I hoped they were all right. When we first started, I kept looking for things to tell Noel and Micah about when we saw them again. I created these elaborate stories in my mind, imagining telling them to Noel and Micah. But for the last day, I hadn't been able to focus on much of anything. I was too tired.

A library, though, that I would have to remember every detail of. But safety came first. We crossed the street, checking all the buildings on the other side until we were back at the beginning. My feet were dragging by then, and my attention was shot. Just the idea of taking a rest seemed to have short-circuited my brain.

The last building we checked was little more than a heap of rubble.

"Let's go check the library. We'll stay there."

Torr nodded, turning to join me in the middle of the street as I started back. He grabbed my arm, pulling me to a stop. "Do you hear that?"

I didn't hear anything. I shook my head, as if somehow that could help me wake up a little more or clear my ears. I listened intently, and then I heard it. It was a cry, a low, pitiful cry. My head shifted from side to side, trying to hone in on its location.

Torr jutted his chin to the right. "I think it's coming from over there."

SADIE HOBBES

I hesitated. Whatever it was, it sounded like it needed help. But could it be a trap? Had some scouts seen us? We hadn't seen anyone, but we were both so tired, I couldn't rule it out.

Another cry removed my hesitation. Without a word, Torr and I moved in the direction of the sound. Some of my exhaustion abated, replaced by adrenaline. The cry came again. It sounded muffled. And desperate.

It was coming from a collapsed house. I craned my neck, trying to see inside. The roof had fallen in, and all four walls had collapsed inward as well. It was now just a pile of rubble, and had been for a while.

I really hoped whoever was making that cry wasn't in there. The cry came again. I turned my head with a frown. The call wasn't coming from inside the rubble, but behind it.

Torr and I split up, each going around the side of the building. My skin felt like it was on fire with prickles of energy racing along it. This was the first time in the last few days that we'd been exposed to any sort of danger. On the bright side, my exhaustion was gone for the moment.

I crept along the side of the building, casting a look inside, but it was still quiet. And there was no way anyone could move around in there without making noise. I rounded the building and came along the back of the house.

There was nothing there. It was just a wide-open space. There wasn't another structure for at least a hundred yards, and the call definitely hadn't been from that far away. Besides, that building looked just as demolished as the first.

Torr appeared on the other side of the house. The sun was just over the horizon now. I glanced over at him and shook my head. But then the cry came again.

My gaze rocketed to a piece of plywood on the ground. It was square, about five feet by five feet. But it couldn't be more than an inch thick, and it was flat on the ground. I doubted even a garter snake could fit under it.

I moved toward it slowly. Torr approached from the other side and reached it first. He knelt down, grabbing the edges. I gave him a nod, and he pulled it back.

A hole in the ground, with a four foot circumference was revealed.

Wind blew hard against my back, shoving my hair forward. I shoved it back in annoyance as I crouched down at the edge of the hole. It looked like an old well. I squinted, trying to see into the well's dark interior.

The small cry came again, followed by a light splash.

"There." Torr pointed down to the far side of the well. I could just make out the outline of a small creature. A fox, may be a dog. But it was trapped down there. It was a good twenty feet down, and the walls looked sheer. I wondered how long the poor guy had been stuck in there. It must've been a while.

"We have to get him out," Torr said.

"It's too narrow for me to fly down. We'll need to use a rope." I slipped off my pack and quickly detached the rope from the side of it. I looked around, but there really wasn't anything to anchor it to.

"I'll take it. You go down. I'll bring you back up," Torr said.

I looked at him. "Are you sure?"

He nodded. "Yeah. I got this."

I didn't waste any more time. I slipped off my sword, then quickly created a loop at the end of the rope and slipped it over my head. I pulled my arms through it so that the knot was in front of me with the rope under my arms.

I made a second loop that reached the base of the first, figuring I could hopefully loop the animal in with me.

As I reached the edge of the hole, the morning light dimmed. I looked up with a frown toward the horizon. It looked as if part of the horizon was now blocked off. "What is that?"

Torr looked over his shoulder toward the horizon. "Uh, whatever it is, we need to hurry before it reaches us."

The wind picked up even more. Dirt particles flew through the air, pelting my skin. "You ready?"

Torr nodded, gripping the rope and bracing his legs. "I've got you. Go."

I carefully eased myself over the side. I held on to the rope while walking down the wall as Torr lowered me down slowly. The walls were packed with dry mud, which made them useless for handholds. Each time my feet touched them, dirt cascaded down. No wonder the poor creature hadn't been able to get out.

The closer I got to the bottom, the clearer the animal became. It looked like it was a dark-brown color. It shivered in water up to its chin. It had to have been standing on two paws. "Hey there. It's okay. I'm coming. I'm coming. I'm almost there."

Now that I was only ten feet away, I could see that it was a dog. The poor thing must have fallen into the well and gotten stuck. It looked up at me, its body totally exhausted, but there was hope in its eyes.

"Hey there, little one. Hold on. I'll get you." I spoke softly and hoped that the little guy was friendly. My boots touch the edges the water.

"Just a little more, Torr," I called up. I sank to the edge of the water and then down to my thighs. "Hold it there."

I got my first good look at the dog. It looked like some sort of pit bull mix. It had a wide face and dark, soft eyes. I couldn't be sure, but I thought his coat was a deep red, and even in the dim light, I could tell its eyes were pale. It was a beautiful dog.

I reached out a hand. "Hey there, buddy. You friendly?"

The dog gave my hand a light lick. And then it tried to move closer to me.

I shifted over toward him. "It's okay, boy. It's okay. Let me come to you."

I slipped both of my legs underneath the dog and then grabbed it by the scruff and pulled it up onto my thighs. The dog, realizing this was its chance, helped by scrambling up my lap. Then it lay against me, all its energy spent.

My legs ached, though. The dog was deceptively heavy. I rubbed its back. "It's okay, baby, I've got you."

With the rope, I looped the other circle I'd made around the dog's shoulders. I'd have to help Torr get us back up. This dog was *heavy*. I leaned my head against the dog's for a minute. It looked up and licked my cheek before burying its head back into my chest.

I smiled at the dog's faith. "What a good boy. Now let's get you out of here."

Leaning my head back and looking toward the top of the hole, I called, "Okay, Torr. I've got him. Let's go."

I grabbed on to the dog with one hand and the rope with the other and then, keeping my feet braced against the wall, slowly began to walk up the wall, trying to keep some of the weight off of the rope.

It wasn't easy. The dog was deadweight resting on my thighs. The poor thing was completely done in.

And I wasn't in much better condition. My thighs burned and my calves ached. Halfway up, my foot slipped. My leg dropped. The back half of the dog did as well. "No!" I grabbed its scruff again, slamming my foot into the wall, my heart pounding.

"Addie?"

"I'm okay. Keep going."

It seemed to take forever, but finally, we reached the edge. I grabbed the dog from underneath its butt and pushed it over the edge of the well. It lay there not moving, just panting hard. Torr kept pulling on the rope, and I managed to get one of my legs over and then rolled over the edge as well.

Now it was my turn to lay panting. God, I had never been so tired in my whole life.

Torr sank to his knees next to the dog.

"It's a girl."

I turned my head slowly. Yes, it was most definitely a girl. A very pregnant one. No wonder she'd been so heavy. Her stomach practically reached her feet. I reached out a hand and gently rubbed the back of the dog's head. "Good girl."

I closed my eyes, about to fall asleep right there.

Torr pushed at my shoulder. "Addie, the sky. Look."

My eyelids cracked open with a frown. The sky seemed to have gotten darker since I'd first gone into the well. I knew I should sit up and see what was going on, but that seemed like so much effort right now. So I simply turned my head to the horizon. Except I couldn't find it.

Fear rolled through me, giving me enough energy to sit up. "What's going on?"

The wind had picked up a lot while I was in the well too. The air seemed to be filled with dirt particles. A stronger gust blew, dislodging debris from the collapsed houses. A few pieces, about a foot long, were flung into the air.

One made a beeline for Torr. He ducked to avoid getting hit. "I think we need to take some cover."

I nodded, rolling slowly to my feet and willing my legs to work. They seriously felt like all the bones had melted.

Torr reached down and picked up the dog. "Come on, girl."

I grabbed my pack and sword, pulling them to me before slinging them over my shoulders. I stumbled at the extra weight. I grabbed the rope, rolling it over my arm as I followed Torr.

Dust and dirt swirled in the air, causing me to squint. I looked behind me. Finally, I could identify what had blocked out the horizon.

A sandstorm. A massive one.

I gripped Torr's shoulder, yelling to be heard over the wind. "Head back to the main street." It was the closest spot with standing buildings.

Torr just nodded, ducking his head and covering the dog's face so she didn't get pelted with the debris. I slipped my pack halfway down my arm, rummaged through, and pulled out a shirt. "Hold on."

I tied the shirt around the lower half of Torr's face so he would be able to breathe better. Then I grabbed the edge of my T-shirt and pulled it up over my nose.

The visibility began to drop dramatically. I could see no more than six inches in front of my face. And even that was rough because I kept shutting my eyes against the dirt. I held on to Torr's shoulder with one hand, worried that if I lost him in this, I'd never be able to find him.

Torr struggled forward with the dog in his arms. I was right behind him, tucking my head down, but it still felt like my face was being scoured. I struggled to come up with a place that we could go. There didn't seem to anything nearby.

Torr stumbled in front of me, dropping to one knee.

I reached out to grab him. I released the edge of my shirt in the process and was rewarded with a face full of sand. It stung as it cut into my skin. "Torr!"

Dust swirled into my mouth as soon as I opened it. I choked, coughing and spluttering while I ducked my head trying to keep any more dust from entering.

Once the coughing had passed, I peeked up, squinting my eyes. I couldn't see any sign of a place that we could take shelter.

Plus, the exhaustion I'd been pushing off was rolling over me, making each step seem more impossible than the last.

Gripping Torr's arm, I pulled him to his feet.

He stumbled forward once again. I stayed right with him. For a moment, I thought maybe we should go back to the abandoned house. Perhaps it would offer at least some protection, although we'd be just as likely to get buried in the thing as protected by it.

In front of me, Torr slammed to a stop. I stumbled into him.

"What?"

He dropped to his knees.

I reached out for him, but he shook his head.

"No, Torr. We have to keep going."

He shook his head. "Can't. Take the dog. Go."

I sank to the ground next to him. "No. I'm not leaving you."

And I realized my mistake as soon as my knees touched the ground. I didn't have the strength to get back up.

Torr fell over to his side. I crawled toward him and pulled the dog toward Torr with the last of my strength. Torr wrapped his arm around the dog, pulling her into his chest to keep her face protected.

I fell over the two of them, trying to protect them the best I could from the storm raging around us. A piece of wood slammed into my back. I let out a little cry that was lost in the wind. The wind tore at my clothes. Sand pelted my exposed skin. I tucked my head down, closed my eyes, and prayed, but I doubted anyone would be listening.

CHAPTER 17

Flashes. All I could see were flashes. I felt someone grab me by the shoulders and pull me up. I landed on a hard surface, but sand was no longer beating against my face, and wind no longer tugged at my clothes. But I could still hear it howling.

I closed my eyes, and the next thing I knew, I got the sense that I was moving. *Torr!* I squinted my eyes open. He lay next to me, his skin browned from the sand.

The dog lay curled up at our feet. I closed my eyes again.

When I flicked them open a short time later, the wind had died down. There was a canvas top above us. A wagon. We were in the back of a wagon. It was closed, keeping out some of the sand. I turned my head, craning to see the front. I could make out the back of someone driving. Their face was covered in cloth, as was every piece of their skin, so I couldn't tell if it was a man or woman, a friend or foe. And right now, I was too exhausted to do anything more than look. My eyes closed again.

The next time they opened, I was still in the wagon. Every part of my body ached, and I knew more than anything I needed to sleep. But I didn't know where we were or who had saved us.

If they had saved us.

For all I knew, they could have some horrible plan for us. I'd heard there were raiders in these parts of the country.

Torr lay next to me, his skin still covered in dust, but the green tint was beginning to show through. I needed to get him out of here before anyone realized what he was.

The dog was no longer in the wagon bed. I sat up, and the world swam for a moment. I grabbed onto the side of the wagon and waited for the dizziness to pass. I reached over and touched Torr's shoulder. "Torr, Torr, wake up," I whispered.

He mumbled something, and then his eyes flickered open before shutting. Then they flickered open wide as he looked around. "Where are we?"

I put my finger to my lips while shaking my head. I reached for my bag and felt my sword there. Whoever had taken us hadn't removed my weapon. It seemed a strange choice.

"If you're awake in there, I could sure use your help," a female voice called from outside the wagon. The voice didn't sound threatening. It actually sounded friendly.

Torr and I exchanged a glance. I put a finger to my lips again. We needed to see how many were out there before we did anything. I slowly crept toward the edge of the wagon and peeked out.

We were in some sort of old garage. Old automotive equipment was strewn around the room. The wind still blew hard against the large windows at the front of the building.

And in the back corner was a woman. She was crouched down low over a mattress. With bright white hair pulled back into a long braid at the base of her neck, she looked up, and green eyes met my gaze. Her face was lined with wrinkles. But also a look of determination. "I could really use your help over here."

My gaze dropped to the ground. On the mattress in front of her lay the dog. Its chest rose and fell quickly.

"She's in labor," the woman said.

I flicked a glance back at Torr and then climbed out of the

wagon. The woman didn't seem like a threat, and she didn't seem at all worried about me or Torr. As I walked over to her, I could tell all her concern was for the dog. In the storm, had she not realized Torr was a demon?

I walked across the garage, skirting around some of the equipment.

The woman gave me a no-nonsense nod.

"Lady here is a little nervous. Do you think you can stay by her head and just pet her to keep her calm while we get through this?"

I moved toward the dog's head, crouching down. "I can do that."

The woman gave her a brisk nod. "That a girl. I'm Vera, by the way."

"Addie. I'm Addie."

Then the two of us didn't say much for the next forty minutes as we helped Lady deliver her pups. There were six pups in all. Each one was tiny and perfect. Lady licked each pup clean as they were held up to her, and then Vera settled them in with their mom before going in and helping the next one out.

Finally, Vera sat back. She wiped her forehead with the back of her hand with a smile. She looked tired but happy. "Well, don't that beat all. I was worried when Lady took off yesterday afternoon. Dogs do that sometimes when they're going into labor. They look for a quiet place. I searched everywhere, but I couldn't find her. I'd gone back home to check and see if she'd come back when I remembered that old well. Then the storm hit, and I thought for sure that I'd lost her. But then I found you two with her. Where'd you find her?"

"In the well."

Vera's eyebrows rose. "How'd you get her out?"

"I climbed down, and my friend pulled us back up."

"Well, you two are a godsend. How's your friend doing? Are you all right? Any injuries?"

I tried to keep the nervousness out of my voice. "No, we're fine. Just a little tired. He's sleeping."

Vera raised an eyebrow. "Really? I thought I heard you two talking in the wagon."

"He woke up for a minute, but he was so exhausted, I told him to go back to sleep."

Vera gave me a smile. "I know what he is. And it's all right. I know he's not like the others."

I stared at her and spoke slowly. "What do you mean?"

Vera pulled out her canteen and took a swig of water. "Why, he's a demon."

"You know?"

"Well, it's kind of hard to miss, even in a sandstorm."

"But why did you help us, then?"

"He hasn't gone through the change yet. So he's not dangerous, or at least, no more dangerous than a human would be to another."

"How do you know that?"

Wings popped out from the woman's back. "Oh, I've seen a thing or two in my long life."

CHAPTER 18

THE WOMAN'S wings were beautiful, soft and gray tinged with pink. "You're ... Are you an angel?"

Vera let out a cackling laugh. "Oh my gods, no. Not an angel. But I am the child of one. Vera Gabriel, at your service. One of the last first-generation Angel Blessed."

At her words, my mouth fell open. A first-generation Angel Blessed? That must mean ... "How old are you?"

"I'll be a hundred and two this year." She winked at me. "I look good for my age."

"Yes, you do. I didn't think there were any more of you around."

"We tend not to advertise. But I'm sure there're one or two besides me left somewhere in the world. We don't have regular meetings or anything, so I can't be sure about that. It's possible I'm the last."

Vera eyed me and raised an eyebrow. "Or maybe I should say, the second to last."

Yet again, I was floored. She knew about Torr, and she knew about me. And she didn't seem bothered by either.

"I can tell you've got quite a bit going on in your life. And I owe you for saving Lady here. Why don't you two come bunk in with me for a little while? From the skyline, I can tell we're in for a few days of bad weather. It's best not to be traveling during those days. And I've got plenty of room and food for you. What do you say?"

I looked toward the wagon and then back at Vera. I didn't sense anything off about the woman. And we certainly hadn't seen anyone else. It was possible it was a trap, but if I was being honest, I was too tired to go down that road. If it was a trap, Torr and I would fight our way out.

"I'll need to ask my friend."

She nodded toward the wagon. "Well, this seems like as good a time as any."

I turned around, shocked to see Torr climbing out the back. I worried about Vera getting a good look at him, but when Torr joined us, Vera merely extended her hand. "I'm Vera."

Torr hesitated for a second, then shook it. "Torr."

"Nice to meet you, Torr. Your friend Addie here tells me you two have been traveling a bit."

Torr nodded, his face not betraying a thing. "Yes." He nodded toward where Lady lay exhausted in the corner, her pups curled up around her. "Is she all right?"

Vera smiled broadly. "Yes, she is, thanks to you two. And now she's the proud mama of six little pups."

Vera glanced out the windows. The storm seemed to have died down a bit. The wind, at least, had quieted. "It looks like the storm's taken a bit of a break. Seems like a good time to make a run for it. I live in the library at the end of the street. You two mind helping me get Lady and her babies settled in the wagon? Then we can head over there and get settled in ourselves before part two of the storm begins. That is, if you two would like to."

I looked at Torr, who gave me a brief nod.

"Okay. Looks like we're going with you."

CHAPTER 19

THE STORM HAD INDEED CALMED down by the time we pulled the wagon out onto Main Street. But by the time we reached the end of the block, the wind had picked up again.

Torr and I sat in the back of the wagon bed with Lady and her puppies,

Torr was right next to Lady. His eyes were wide as he looked at the little pups feeding from their mom. For the first time since I'd met Torr, he seemed relaxed. He wasn't worried about something. He was completely and totally enamored with the pups in front of him.

Vera pulled the wagon to a stop and hustled around to the back, pulling open the gate. "We better get moving. It's getting bad again. Can you take the pups? I'll get Lady."

I nodded, carefully taking three of the puppies from Lady. I wrapped the pups in blankets to keep them warm and protect them from the wind. Torr did the same with the other three.

I worried Lady might become aggressive at the move, but she was so exhausted, she barely batted an eye. Vera reached in and gently pulled Lady to her chest before she hustled toward the front of the library.

Climbing from the wagon, I kept my head down, the pups tucked into me. The wind once again tugged at my clothes, sand scalding my face. Vera held the door open.

Torr and I slipped inside. I let out a breath as the door closed behind us, grateful to be inside.

I wasn't sure what to expect of the library, being that Vera apparently used it as her home.

But the first floor looked just like a library. There was a gleaming circulation desk straight in front of us. Rows and rows of books lined the shelves on either side. There were even display tables in front that had books arranged by topic. And the whole place was spotless. Besides what we'd dragged in, it didn't look like there was a speck of dust anywhere.

Vera must have read the amazement on my face. She gave me a shrug. "I like to keep things clean. And libraries, well, they should always be protected. If you two are up for it, let's head to the third floor. That's where I set up camp."

My legs threatened to revolt at the idea of three sets of stairs, but I followed her. Torr stopped at the base, readjusted the pups in his arms, and with a sigh, began to climb. The stairwell looked out into a courtyard, where Vera had set up crops. She had put a covering over them, which hopefully would keep them partially protected from the ravages of the storm.

A quick glance at the second floor as we passed showed more rooms filled with stacks of books. I couldn't help but think of how Noel would be ecstatic to be in a place like this.

The thought of Noel pulled my emotions down, so I quickly shied away from it. Now wasn't the time.

Vera hustled to the third floor. She stepped onto the landing and headed down the hall to the left. "This way, this way."

We passed a large room that had been turned into a living room of sorts. Tall wooden bookcases stood against the back walls. A mix of chairs and couches had been brought in, along with some side tables and lamps. A pair of deep-red drapes framed the two windows that overlooked the main street.

Next to the living room was a kitchen. A stainless steel counter ran along the back wall, bracketed by a small refrigerator and cupboard of cups, plates, and bakeware. A large butcher block island stood in front of the counter. A table and four chairs sat against a row of windows framed by cheerful blue drapes with yellow sunflowers on them. Sunflowers had been painted along the walls as well.

But Vera passed all of these, still carrying Lady. She headed down the hallway, and we passed two bedrooms, one on either side of the hall. Both were small but clean, each with a brown poster bed and clean white linens under floral quilts.

Vera bustled into the second door on the right. It was slightly larger than the other two and had a desk in the corner along with a small bookcase filled with books and old photos.

Nestled in the corner was a well-used dog bed. Gently, Vera lay Lady down. "There you go, Mama."

Torr and I carefully handed each of the puppies to Vera, who placed them close to their mom. And then once they were all settled, she stood up and smiled. "Don't that beat all." She looked over at us and grinned. "Well, I think we could all use something to eat."

Torr's stomach grumbled in response.

Vera laughed. "I'll take that as agreement. I'm just going to run down and take care of the horses."

"Do you need help?" I asked even as my legs threatened to quit if forced back down and up those stairs again.

"No, I'm just going to put them up real quick. If you guys want, there's a bathroom at the end of the hall. Water's warm. You could grab a quick shower and get cleaned up.

The mention of a shower made the dryness of my skin feel even worse. The idea of getting all this sand off of me sounded like heaven.

I looked at Torr, who sat next to Lady, his hand resting on her head. He looked perfectly content where he was. He wasn't even a little bit worried about Vera. His relaxation put me at ease.

"That would be great."

Vera directed me to the washroom at the end of the hall and then told me to come find her in the kitchen when I was done.

The shower was warm, which was a blessing. But I didn't stay in long. I quickly got cleaned up and put on a change of clothes, my only change of clothes. I stopped in and told Torr the bathroom was free if he wanted it. He shot a longing glance at the pups before standing with a sigh.

I smiled as I left him to it and made my way to the kitchen.

Vera turned around from the counter as I walked in. "Well, you look refreshed."

"And I feel it. Thank you."

"No thanks needed. Lady would be in a lot of trouble if it weren't for you two. Soup should be ready in just about ten minutes."

"Smells good." And it did. My mouth was practically watering.

"There's some water on the table there. Help yourself," Vera said as she chopped up potatoes.

I did, and after the first glass, I realized just how thirsty I was. I downed the glass and poured myself a second. Then I just sat watching Vera, almost mesmerized by her movements. After being on the move for so long, being able to just sit was its own kind of heaven.

I studied the woman across from me. She was dicing potatoes with a practiced ease and then dropping them into the steaming pot. No alarm bells were going off around her. And the fact that she hadn't been scared of Torr, well, that said legions, but it also left me with lots of questions. "Vera, can I ask you something?"

"Shoot." Two more potatoes into the pot.

"Back at the garage, you said you knew Torr wasn't a threat even though you knew he was a demon. How come?"

"He hasn't gone through the change."

"'The change'? What does that mean?"

Vera grabbed a towel and wiped her hands as she leaned back against the counter. "What do you know about demons?"

I shook my head. "Not much. I mean, I know when they appear, they try to kill humans. And I know that Torr isn't like them."

"They don't just try to kill humans. Sometimes they *take* humans. And those they take they try to initiate into their ranks. But they can't simply conscript them. There is a critical step that must happen during the process that will allow them to become a full-fledged demon."

I leaned forward, even though I had a feeling I knew what she was going to say.

"They have to take a human life. And they have to do it in cold blood. It can't be an accident or mistake. They have to *intend* to kill. Torr hasn't done that. So he is, in essence, simply a green human."

"So he *is* a human? Was he captured and taken down there?"

"He doesn't know?"

I shook my head. "I don't think so. He doesn't really talk about that type of stuff."

"I'm actually not sure about that part. I think the demons reproduce, but I'm not sure. But I've seen others like him in the past. Not full-fledged demons. They look like demons in many ways, but they don't have that edge. In fact, I used to have a good friend, he passed away years ago now, but he was like your friend Torr. He was a good man. I miss him."

I stared at her in shock. There were other people out there like Torr? He wasn't the only one? "Why have I never heard about this?"

"The knowledge has been around, but like many things, it sort of drifted away. People knew about them during the Angel War, but there weren't a lot of them. And to be perfectly honest, as soon as people saw green skin, they went in for the kill. Torr is lucky that you were the one who came across him and not someone else. Do you really think anyone else would have given him a chance to explain?"

I pictured the Seraph Force and the people of Sterling Peak. They were so sure that demons were evil that there was no questioning, there was just fighting.

Vera turned back to the stove. "Looks like we're about ready here. Can you grab some bowls?" She nodded toward the shelving on the right-hand side of the room.

I stood up, my legs shaking a little. I really needed to rest. I grabbed the bowls and walked over.

Torr, sniffing like a bloodhound, appeared in the doorway. "That smells delicious."

I tensed. Now that Torr was clean, his demon nature was completely obvious.

But Vera didn't bat an eye.

"Well, I hope it tastes as good as it smells." She quickly ladled the soup into bowls, and then we took a seat at the table.

Torr gobbled down two bowls before he finally sat back. "That was delicious. Thank you."

Vera grinned, only halfway through her first bowl. "It's good to have someone to cook for."

Torr patted his belly. "And I appreciate it."

"We both do." I broke off some bread and dunked it in my stew. Right now, I was so content, it was hard to keep my eyes open. For the first time since we'd left Sterling Peak, I didn't feel the unending urge to move.

Vera's gaze strayed to the window. The storm raged against it, making it difficult to see outside. "Looks like the storm's going to last a few days. You two are welcome to bunk here until it passes. I have an entire room dedicated to the Angel War downstairs. Might help answer some your questions." She looked at me.

I glanced over at Torr and could read the hope in his eyes. He liked Vera. He wanted to stay.

And surprisingly, I found that I wanted to as well. There was something extremely comforting about her. Torr could be himself, and she didn't seem to want anything from us.

And the idea of just staying in one place for a little while was too tempting to resist. But it wouldn't be fair to Vera if we kept her in the dark about the stakes. "You sure won't be any bother? There *is* someone who will come looking for us. He's powerful. He's got the Seraph Force looking for us as well."

Vera shrugged. "I figured as much. You'll be safe here. No one ever comes here."

I knew it was wishful thinking, but I believed her. I smiled. "Then I think we'd like to take you up on your offer. We'll stay."

"Excellent. It'll be good to have the company."

Torr smiled as he reached for some more bread. And I realized that for the first time since the archangel had arrived, we might have caught a break.

CHAPTER 20

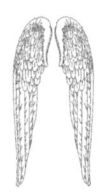

NOEL

The wind howled as Noel grabbed Micah's hand. "Run, Micah, run!"

The two of them tore down the alleyway. The steps behind them only got louder.

Noel shot a glance over her shoulder. The demon drew closer. It was immense, the biggest one she'd ever seen.

Her heart rate spiked. It was too big, too fast. They'd never be able to outrun it.

A shadow dropped from the building above them. It slammed into the back of the demon. Addie rolled to her feet, a flaming sword in front of her. With two quick slashes of it, she destroyed the demon. It fell in pieces in the alley around her before it was reduced to ashes.

Holding the sword in one hand, she extended her other to Noel. "Come with me."

Noel grabbed Addie's hand. "Thank God. We've been looking for you."

Addie tightened her grip around Noel's hand, yanking her forward painfully.

Noel stared down at the hand and then up into Addie's face, which morphed in front of her very eyes. Her face grew wider as her skin darkened to green. Her eyes sunk deeper into her skull and began to glow a bright red.

"You should have listened to them." The voice that came out of Addie's mouth was hers but different: deeper, crueler. She raised her sword.

Noel's eyes flew open. Her arm swung up. Donovan reared back to avoid getting hit. Noel stared at him, her heart still pounding. The image of demon Addie was at the forefront of her mind.

"Good. You're awake. I've been trying to wake you for the last two minutes," Donovan whispered.

Her breath still coming out in pants, Noel looked over at the bed, where Tess was stuffing some clothes into a pack. "What's going on?"

Donovan indicated that she should whisper. He lowered his own voice. "We need to get you two out of here. It's not safe for you guys anymore."

Noel clambered out of the bed. "Why? What happened?"

"The scouts returned and have nothing to report. They've seen no sign of Addie. Graham went into a rage. He's up at the Academy making plans. We need to get you two out of here before he gets back."

Tess walked over and handed Noel a pack. "This one's for you."

"Where's Micah?"

"Bathroom." The sound of running water came from inside.

"Where are we going?" Noel asked as she slipped the pack over her shoulders.

"Not sure yet." Donovan cast his eyes around as if looking for someone hiding in the corners. "The first priority is just getting you guys out of Sterling Peak and away from Graham."

"And D'Angelo," Tess muttered.

Noel pictured the man who'd interrupted their training session, the one who'd tried to arrest her and Micah before Addie had stopped him. "What's going on with D'Angelo?"

"Graham made him second-in-command. Graham is going out searching for Addie tomorrow. And he's leaving D'Angelo in charge."

"But I thought you were next in command," Micah said as he exited the bathroom.

Donovan just shrugged.

Tess handed Micah the bag she'd been packing. "He's supposed to be. But Graham demoted him. D'Angelo is now in charge of the Seraph Force."

"But if Graham's going to be out there, shouldn't we stay here?" Noel asked.

Donovan shook his head. "I don't trust D'Angelo either. And I certainly don't want you guys near him. Graham and his forces are leaving first thing in the morning."

"D'Angelo is power hungry," Tess said. "We don't know what he'll do. Which is why we're leaving now."

Donovan took Noel gently by the arm and prodded her toward the door. "Come on. We need to get moving."

Once Donovan reached the door, he peered down the hallway. He gave a nod and stepped outside. Noel followed, then Micah and Tess brought up the rear. Quickly they made their way down the stairs. Voices reached them from the hall.

Marcus, who'd been waiting in the foyer, hurried over to the hallway toward the voices, holding a large stack of books. Seconds later, the sound of the books hitting the floor could be heard. "My goodness. How clumsy of me. Would you mind helping me?"

There was some grumbling as somebody helped Marcus pick up his books. Donovan gave a nod, and the four of them scampered across the foyer and out the front door. They hurried outside and hopped into the waiting security cart with Sheila behind the wheel. Without a word, she took off, heading quickly for the bridge.

Noel glanced back at the house, her heart pounding, but no alarm went off. No shouts followed them. The streets were quiet. Darkness had settled in.

Sheila quickly drove them onto the bridge, waving off the guards as they made their way to the other side, which was dark. She stopped near the edge, turned the cart off, and stepped out onto the bridge. Everyone quickly followed. Part of the bridge was already retracted, but a plank had been placed across the gap.

"D'Angelo's orders," Sheila said. "The bridge is to be closed every night for the foreseeable future."

Noel felt anger burn inside her. That would protect the people of Sterling Peak while leaving the people of Blue Forks completely exposed.

"You guys are going to need to climb across. Be careful," Sheila said.

Donovan extended his hand. "Thanks, Sheila."

Sheila nodded, returning the handshake. "Just take care of these two." Then she turned and hugged Noel and Micah. She looked down at the two of them. "Look after each other, okay?"

They both nodded back at her. Noel felt a catch in her throat. Without Addie, she'd thought she and Micah were alone in all of this. But it looked like they still had people here who cared about them.

Sheila quickly got back in the cart and headed back across the bridge.

"I'll go first." Tess tightened the straps on her pack and then carefully walked across the plank, keeping her arms out for balance.

Noel followed her, not letting herself look down. Micah walked nimbly across, and then Donovan followed last. When he reached the other side, he kicked the end of the plank. It tumbled to the river below with a splash.

Noel looked over the edge, realizing he had just cut all their ties with Sterling Peak. She looked up at Donovan and Tess. They were risking a lot by helping them, and not just their status. Because if Marcus was right about what Graham would do to fulfill his mission, they were risking their very lives.

CHAPTER 21

ADDIE

Dust swirled up in the air as I closed the book in my lap. I coughed, waving my hand in front of my face. Then I rubbed my eyes, which felt as dry as the sandstorm had been.

Torr and I had agreed to stay with Vera for a few days, but somehow a few days had stretched into a week. At first, I figured we needed the rest. Then I justified it by saying I didn't want to pull Torr away from the puppies and that it gave me a chance to research the Angel War.

But the truth was, we both just liked being around Vera. She was always cooking for us or telling us stories from her long life. And she shared what she knew about demons and the Angel War, although she admitted it had been a long time since she'd really thought about either.

"Those books really haven't had much use in the last few years," Vera said from across the room.

Today she and Torr had joined me in searching for more information on the Angel War and, more specifically, what exactly had led to its start.

No one seemed to understand why the war had begun. It seemed as if one day the demons just appeared in huge legions, and then the archangels arrived. But what had allowed the demons to escape hell in such large numbers was still a complete mystery.

"Well, I think I'm about done reading for the day," Vera said. "My eyes feel like they're going to bleed. And I could use a little something to eat. How about you?"

I nodded, my stomach growling in response. "That would be great. How about if I cook tonight? You've done enough."

Vera shook her head with a smile. "Oh, I don't mind. It's nice to cook for other people for a change."

Vera was definitely a better cook, so I didn't put up too much of a fight. And I had to admit, Vera did seem pretty happy that we were here. She'd been on her own for years, except for occasional supply runs. Pitkin had been hit by an illness a few decades back. Most of the town had died, including Vera's husband and son. For a few years, the remaining townspeople had stayed on. But one by one, they left until it was just Vera.

She stood, wiping her hands on her pants. "Well, I'm going to go get dinner started. You mind checking on Lady for me?"

I nodded, marveling as Vera hustled out of the room. I had no idea where Vera got all of her energy. She had the energy of someone a quarter of her age.

Maybe that was what I had to look forward to: a future of unbridled energy. If, of course, I had a future. I shoved that maudlin thought away. I'd done a pretty good job of keeping Graham and the threat he represented out of my mind, or at least only lurking at the back end of it for the last few days.

But every once in a while, an image of him would flash through my mind, causing my pulse to race. I'd imagine the feel of his lips on mine.

No, stop it. That's not helping. Once again, I forced the image from my mind.

It was quickly replaced with an image of Noel and Micah. God, I missed them so much. And I hated that I left without saying goodbye.

I banished them from my mind too, but the ache of loss lingered nonetheless.

I tried not to let out a groan as I stood up. My back ached from being hunched over for so long. It hadn't really seemed to bother Vera at all. Apparently, that particular skill was not in my bag of inherited bonuses from Daddy.

Vera's existence, though, did make me wonder how many other true Angel Blessed might still be out there. And my own existence made me wonder if maybe some other angels had wandered around for "a weekend of fun," as Donovan had put it.

The thought of Donovan, of course, led to thoughts of Graham again. And my heart ached. I was ridiculous. The man wanted me dead, yet here I was, looking for reasons to excuse that behavior or believe I'd misunderstood it.

I had turned into a cliché, a very needy, pathetic one.

I wandered down the hall and stopped in at the room that we had set up as the nursery. I was unsurprised to see Torr sitting leaning against the back wall with Lady's head in his lap as he read another book on the Angel War. A puppy, brown with white paws, was curled up in the crook of his arm. Another lay in his lap, this one with a large white spot on his back. The other four, all a mix of brown and white, were spread around Lady, snoozing.

Torr had completely and hopelessly fallen in love with Lady and all her pups. He might have never been around a dog before, but he was certainly making up for lost time. He looked up, a peaceful look on his face. I don't think I'd ever seen him look that content before. He smiled at me. "Hey."

"Hey yourself." I walked over and sat down, gently running a hand over Lady's head as she opened her eyes, her tail thumping before she closed them again.

The poor new mama was pretty tired these days. Not that I could blame her. It took a lot to look after this crew of six.

I scooped up a puppy and placed her in my lap and sat down. "Find anything?"

Torr nodded toward the book. "It's not really shedding any new light on a timeline, but the stories of the battles are pretty interesting."

I knew what he meant. I had read more than my fair share of those battle tales as well. And they were intriguing. The abilities of some of the archangels had been phenomenal: strength, speed, fighting prowess. It was easy to see why they had won against the demons.

"I don't get why the demons even bothered. There was no chance they were going to be able to defeat the angels."

Torr shrugged. "Maybe they didn't expect the angels to arrive. Maybe they figured the angels would kind of stay out of it. It's not like they'd been out on Earth very often."

I had to admit that was true. "But being the angels did intercede, why would they be increasing their numbers again now? They have to expect the same thing to happen."

"Maybe they know something we don't."

I nodded feeling a chill. Maybe they did. Maybe this time they believed things were going to be different.

And maybe humanity would suffer the way the demons had intended the first time round.

CHAPTER 22

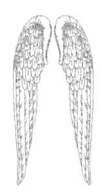

NOEL

Noel ran. She could feel the shadows encroaching on her. No matter how fast she was, she couldn't outrun them.

She looked around for Micah, but she couldn't see him at all. She needed to find Addie. If she found Addie, everything would be all right. But where was she?

Reaching the end of the path, she stumbled over an exposed root. The shadows saw their chance and swooped in. One grabbed her by the shoulder. Noel opened her mouth and screamed.

Noel's eyes flew open, her hand rolled into a fist, and she swung out wildly.

Donovan dodged back, blocking her left fist, but just barely. "Whoa, whoa. Seriously, do you try to punch everybody that wakes you up, or is it just me?"

Noel's heart galloped. She stared wildly around, seeing Micah looking at her with big eyes from over by the horses, where he was helping Tess. "Sorry."

Donovan looked down at her. "Are you all right?"

Noel nodded, not looking at his face. It was just a dream, another nightmare. Since Addie left, it seemed every time she closed her eyes, she had them. "I'm fine. It just wasn't a great sleep."

"I don't think any of us had that." He reached out a hand. The dream still had a hold of her. A chill swept over her skin. She gave a shudder before reaching up and grasping Donovan's hand. He easily pulled her to her feet. "We need to get going. We probably shouldn't have slept for so long, but I think we all needed it."

"You still thinking he's looking for us?"

"Even before the archangel, Graham was tenacious. I doubt that's changed."

Noel nodded and took the piece of jerky he offered and then took a bite. She chewed mechanically, not even tasting it. They had driven hard for the last five days, barely stopping. They'd needed to get as much distance between themselves and Graham as possible.

Even so, they had barely avoided a patrol two days ago, part of the early scouts sent out looking for Addie. They could easily report back seeing them when they returned. So instead of relaxing after three days of brutal travel, they had picked up their pace.

But they had no destination in mind. They knew they couldn't go anywhere that Graham would know people. And Donovan and Graham knew all the same people. Tess had her family back in Chicago, but Chicago was still one of the more populated cities. So that was on the backburner for now. Right now, putting distance between themselves and Graham was the only goal.

Noel and Micah had never been anywhere beyond the West Coast. And even then, it had only been the orphanage and Blue Forks. It was strange seeing new landscapes. Yesterday, they'd left green hills behind, heading into much more barren territory. There weren't any trees, only scraggly bushes. But there was something appealing about all that open space.

The sleeping accommodations definitely left something to be desired, though. Noel's back ached from sleeping on the hard ground, but she didn't complain. She merely rolled up her bedroll and after tying the straps, headed to the horse she and Tess had shared yesterday.

Tess looked at her over the back of the horse. "How you doing?"

Noel just shrugged. She didn't really know how to answer that. Unsettled? Cast adrift? Either of them would be accurate. But she couldn't say that. She couldn't give voice to what she was feeling inside. So she locked it all down and glanced over at Micah. "Did you eat?"

"Yeah, I had some jerky. It's horrible."

Donovan laughed. "You'll need to grow a taste for it, I'm afraid."

Micah grimaced. Noel let herself smile. "So where are we heading?"

Tess and Donovan exchanged glances, and then Tess said, "We'll head toward New Chicago. It's populated, but I think I can get word to some people who can help us."

Noel nodded, even though that strange gnawing sensation had appeared in her stomach again. She didn't think they were supposed to go New Chicago. But she also didn't know how to explain what she was feeling.

She gripped the canteen and walked over to the edge of the small rise. They were tucked into the side of a large hill. It gave them a good view if anyone was going to try and sneak up on them and also gave them an escape route through the back hills.

Tess came and stood next to her a few seconds later. "Everything's ready. We should get going. It'll be daylight soon."

Noel nodded, still looking out over the landscape. "What's over that way?"

Tess frowned, glancing at where Noel was looking. "I'm not

sure, exactly. A bunch of small towns, I guess. Most of them are probably abandoned."

Noel stared off in the distance, a strange sort of certainty taking hold of her. "We need to go that way."

Tess's eyebrows rose. "Why?"

Noel shook her head. "I can't explain it. I just know we're supposed to go that way." She looked up at Tess. "I think that's where Addie is."

Tess studied her face for a long moment. "I know you want to find Addie and Torr, but this country is huge. They could be anywhere. They could have taken off in absolutely any direction."

Noel knew that Tess was right. But the more she stared off into the distance, the more certain she became that Addie was somewhere to the east of them. Going north would only pull them farther away from her.

Noel didn't know how she knew, but she did. She was absolutely certain of it. "No, she's there. I know it."

Tess stared at Noel and then looked off in the distance. She let out a sigh.

"We don't actually have a destination in mind, right?" Noel pressed.

"No, not exactly," Tess admitted.

"It wouldn't hurt to go check out what's over there, would it?"

Tess let out a sigh. "*One* day. We'll head in that direction for one day. But if we don't see any sign of them, we need to start heading north."

Noel smiled. "Great. Thanks, Tess."

"Don't thank me yet. We don't know what's in that direction. Out here, things aren't as nice and organized as they are in Blue Forks, so you and Micah need to do everything we say, okay?"

Noel nodded. "You got it."

Tess glanced over her shoulder. "Well, I'll go break the news to Donovan. He's not going to be thrilled."

As Tess headed back for the horses, Noel turned back toward the distance. Something was definitely pulling her in that direction. Addie was that way. She didn't know how, but down deep, she knew they'd find her there.

CHAPTER 23

ADDIE

THE TOP FLOOR of the library had a small hatch that led to the attic roof. After a scrumptious dinner of eggplant rollatini, I wandered up there. I needed a little time to think.

The more I thought about the reasons for running, the more it became unreal to me. Maybe this really *had* all been a mistake. Maybe Marcus had misunderstood the translation. After all, it was a mistake in translation that led to everything to begin with.

Maybe I had misunderstood what I'd seen at the bridge. Maybe the scouts had misunderstood Graham's orders.

Maybe, maybe, maybe.

I wandered the rooftop and then settled in at the small overhang that Vera had created. There was a chair and a large dog bed. Apparently, she and Lady escaped up here regularly. I wiped the sand off the chair and shook out the dog bed before taking a seat. There was a telescope up here too, but I ignored it for now.

Had I really gone off on this mad dash across the country based on little more than Marcus's words and a cold glance from

Graham? But then there had been the scouts. But maybe they'd misinterpreted why Graham was looking for me.

I dropped my head into my hands. Right, everyone was misinterpreting things. How likely was that? I just wish I knew what my next move should be.

The books hadn't revealed much about the beginnings of the Angel War or the prophecy. And even in the ones that addressed either, the authors seemed to be guessing. One author argued there'd been a war in Hell that forced the demons out. Another maintained that the demons had finally reached a large enough population that they felt they could take over Earth.

A third even argued the demons were really aliens and had escaped back to their home planet at the end of the Angel War. Crazier and crazier the theories got, but none seemed any more likely than the next.

As for the prophecy, everyone during the Angel War kept looking for signs that it was about to come true. Every time a child showed angelic abilities, the speculation began. But then years passed, the prophecy wasn't realized, and it faded from the conversation.

And if the people writing the books on the Angel War didn't have the answers, reading them seemed like an exercise in futility.

But what else could I do? Should I go back to Blue Forks and see what was going on? Should I stay here?

I had to admit it was nice staying here. Vera accepted Torr, so he could just wander around being himself. The puppies were definitely a bonus.

But I knew that we couldn't stay here indefinitely. I even entertained the idea of going back to Blue Forks, grabbing Noel and Micah, and returning here with them. That would be better than leaving them with Graham if something was wrong.

But it was only a matter of time before Graham caught up with me. I couldn't put more targets in his way. And I certainly couldn't repay Vera's hospitality by making her one. We'd already been here too long.

I stood and walked along the edge of the roof again. The truth was, I was still having trouble accepting what Marcus had said, even though it had spurred me on this journey. The further in time we got from that conversation, the more unreal it seemed. I knew Graham. He was a good man. There was no way that Marcus could be right.

The hatch to the roof opened, and Vera appeared. She smiled as she spied me. "I thought you might be up here. It's a good spot for after dinner."

I looked behind her, but Torr didn't appear.

Vera noted my look. "He doesn't seem to want to leave those puppies. I was thinking maybe he should keep one of them. He seems like a boy who should have a dog."

I knew Torr would love that. But I didn't even know where we would be in a few days, so I definitely couldn't commit to it. "Maybe."

Vera joined me at the edge, looking out over the old town. "You thinking of going back out again?"

I sighed. "Is it that obvious?"

Vera let out one of her cackling laughs. "Well, it doesn't take a psychic to see that you're missing your family something fierce. And the fact that we haven't found any answers is probably making you question why you're even here."

I studied her, wondering if some sort of telepathy was part of her bag of angel tricks. "Well, that's about right."

"I understand that. It's hard when you haven't been around the archangels to understand what they're capable of."

"I just … I just keep thinking that maybe I misunderstood what I saw. Maybe I should have talked to Graham, that I should have given him a chance to explain what happened with the archangel."

There was quiet for a moment before Vera spoke. "The angels aren't like us. I think you were right to run, Addie.

Because it would have been a fight between you and this man of yours. And you wouldn't have it in you to hurt him. But he wouldn't have had the ability to *keep* from hurting you. And I don't think that's changed just because time's moved on a little bit."

I knew she was right. I was just clinging to the idea that everything was a big misunderstanding because I wanted it to be one. I wanted to go back and have a life where Graham was part of it. I didn't want to be on the run. I wanted to have Noel and Micah and Donovan and Tess and everybody else around me.

"It's never easy, child. Life wasn't meant to be. I think that's why you got free will. So that you can make these choices and decide for yourself what's best for you and for those in your life. So let me ask you, if you went back, and if Graham tried to kill you, would you be able to kill him?"

I recoiled from the very idea of it. I shook my head. "No. But maybe I wouldn't have to. I'm stronger than he is. I have more abilities than he does."

"Maybe. But he doesn't have emotions to worry about. He could hurt anyone and anything to get you to do what he wanted. Is there anyone back there that you would lay down your life for?"

Visions of Noel and Micah floated through my mind.

Vera read the answer on my face. "He could use them against you. Being away makes it safer for them, but I'm sure you'll see them again. Life has a funny way of working out."

Vera walked over to the old telescope. She pulled out her rag and started cleaning the dust off of it, fiddling with the knobs as she looked through the viewer.

I stared out over the empty town, wondering about what she had said. Could I truly risk Noel and Micah's lives just to sate my curiosity?

Maybe I could send Torr in, and he could get the lay of the land?

I discarded the thought almost as soon as I had it. I couldn't risk him like that. For all I knew, the archangel had given Graham the ability to see Torr.

Finished cleaning off the telescope, Vera peered through it, but instead of aiming at the sky, she aimed it at the land surrounding us.

Looking for a distraction from my thoughts, I wandered over to her. "See anything good?"

Vera pulled back from the viewfinder. "Take a look for yourself. I like to keep an eye on the surrounding area. Every once in a while, some raiders or some bad weather comes along. This helps me be prepared."

I scanned the land, turning the telescope as I did. It was on a swivel, making it easier. There wasn't much out there. Everything seemed to be pretty quiet.

Then I spied a cloud of dust kicking up somewhere in the distance. "What's that?"

Vera peered through the telescope as I stepped away from it. She frowned. "Looks like some raiders. They're moving pretty fast." She swung the telescope a little farther to the left and then stopped. "Looks like they're going after someone. Two horses. Three, maybe four, people on them." Vera stepped back. "It doesn't look like they're going to be able to escape them."

"These raiders," I said quietly, "what will they do if they catch them?"

"Take everything the people have."

"So just rob them?"

Vera shook her head. "No. They'll take *everything* those people have, including their lives."

CHAPTER 24

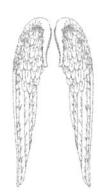

NOEL

TESS LEANED FORWARD over the neck of the horse. Noel grabbed onto her waist, praying for them to go faster. Donovan and Micah raced next to them on a second horse.

But both the horses had already been tired from nearly a week of heavy riding. Plus, unlike the group following them, they both carried two people instead of one. Now both animals were frothing at the mouth.

Two of the raiders were coming up fast behind them. They seemed to have come out of nowhere. At first, Donovan and Tess wanted to fight them, but as the numbers had grown, they'd known that fighting wasn't an option. There were too many of them. And while Tess and Donovan could no doubt protect themselves, Noel knew that they were worried about protecting her and Micah.

Swallowing, Noel darted another look behind her. The raiders seemed to be gaining on them. Their faces were covered in dirt. But more than one of them was smiling as if looking forward to what was to come.

Noel didn't know what to do. She didn't know how to help. At the same time, she knew there was nothing she could do. All she had left was prayer.

But prayer had never really worked well for her before.

Donovan moved his horse closer to them. "After the rise?"

Tess nodded. "Yes."

Up ahead was a large outcropping of rocks. If they could get on top of the rocks, they would have the higher ground, which could give them a small advantage.

Tess yelled over her shoulder, "When I stop the horse, you grab Micah, and you sprint up to the top of those boulders, you hear me?"

"Yeah," she yelled back, her whole body tense.

They raced on. The boulders loomed closer.

A little more than a dozen feet from the boulder, Tess yanked the horse to a stop.

Noel flung herself from the back of the horse, rolling as she hit the ground, and dashed over to Donovan. Micah slid off the back of his horse, his knees wobbling as he touched down.

She grabbed his hand before he even had his feet under him and half carried, half pulled him toward the boulders. Tess and Donovan stayed on their horses. They pulled their swords from their sheaths and turned to face the oncoming group.

Noel bypassed the first boulder, which was too sheer to climb. She hurried toward the second, which was only about four feet tall. She pushed Micah toward it, and he scrambled up it like a little squirrel. Micah had always been good at climbing. Noel quickly followed him.

By the time she reached the top, he'd already climbed up two more boulders. He now stood about ten feet from the ground.

"Get back from the edge," she ordered him as she pulled her knife from its sheath and held it in front of her.

The crash of metal signaled that Tess and Donovan had

already engaged the raiders. Her head jolted up as she watched three raiders hit the ground. Another two quickly followed.

But then something hit Tess on the side of her chest as she jabbed at another raider. Her arm extended, she lost her balance and tumbled from her perch. Donovan was dropped to the ground almost at the same time.

Noel's heart caught in her throat as she watched them take the raiders on from the ground. They were holding their own, but Noel quickly realized that there were even more than she had originally thought. There were at least another fifteen still on horseback.

She swallowed hard, knowing that even Donovan and Tess couldn't beat those odds.

CHAPTER 25

ADDIE

The raiders were getting closer. From this distance, I couldn't make out exactly who it was they were chasing. I couldn't even tell much beyond the fact that there were two horses. I looked up at Vera. "Any chance that the raiders are going after someone who deserves it?"

Vera shook her head. "They're not Seraph Force. They go after people and get what they want. Man, woman, child, it doesn't matter to them. And they don't have compassion for the people they go against."

I stared at the rising dust. I'd made a concerted effort to keep a low profile since Torr and I left Sterling Peak. I didn't want anyone reporting back that we'd been seen. If I went out there, someone would talk. And I liked where Torr and I were right now. I liked being with Vera.

I sighed as my wings extended behind me. But my comfort was nothing compared to somebody else's life.

Vera stepped back with a smile. "Been a while since I've seen a pair of young ones. Happy hunting."

Without another word, I took off into the air. As much as I had resisted flying these last couple of days, I couldn't help but admit that I had missed it. Flying had become my natural state. I felt free. I felt like me.

But all those thoughts were on a parallel track to my other concerns: the raiders advancing on those two horses. I didn't engulf my wings in flames, hoping that maybe that might attract a little less attention.

I nearly rolled my eyes at the thought, as if somehow a flying woman would be less distracting than a flying woman with flaming wings.

By the time I reached the back of the raiders group, the front of the pack had already engaged the horsemen. I swooped down, and with my wings out wide, knocked raiders right off the backs of their horses. I swept through, knocking and kicking them from their perches. A few took one look at me and pulled on the reins of their horses and bolted away.

I sighed. So much for remaining incognito.

One of the raiders that I dislodged came at me with a machete in his hands. I slipped to the side, yanking on his arm and continuing the sweep of his movements, impaling the machete in his collarbone.

He screamed and dropped to the ground. A second one tried to sneak up behind me. I slammed a back kick into his stomach before turning with a jumping round kick to his face.

A few more decided their chances were better on the open ground and took off at a fast clip. The two people who'd been on horses at the front dispatched the last two raiders with a sweep of their swords.

I stared at them, my mouth falling open. "Donovan? Tess?"

CHAPTER 26

NOEL

Noel couldn't believe her eyes.

It was Addie.

She'd seen the speck in the distance and had thought at first it was a bird. But then the "bird" grew larger and larger until Addie came into view.

She started taking out raiders at the back of the pack. Noel had stood transfixed as she watched her fight. She'd never seen Addie fight with wings before. It was a sight to behold. She truly looked like a warrior angel.

Micah moved next to her. "Is that... Addie?"

Noel grabbed his hand, squeezing it tight, staring at Addie as she took down one after another of the raiders. She was amazing.

A hand clamped onto her ankle and yanked. Noel crashed to the ground but managed to throw out her palms. She tucked her chin so the back of her skull didn't slam into the rock face.

Distracted by Addie's appearance, she hadn't noticed the raider climbing up the rocks. He leered at her over the top of the rock face, showing a mouth full of rotted yellow teeth.

Noel slammed the heel of her boot into his face three times. His head jerked back, and he disappeared from view.

Micah grabbed her by the shoulders and pulled her back from the edge. "You okay?"

Noel nodded, scrambling back to her feet. She crept toward the edge and peered over. The man who'd grabbed her lay sprawled on the ground below, grimacing in pain. He'd landed on a sharp rock.

Her gaze turned from the man, who was no longer a danger, to Addie as she approached Donovan and Tess.

Then Addie's gaze shifted. She looked straight at Noel and Micah. Her mouth fell open. A smile burst across her face. She was in the air and across the space in no time, landing directly in front of them and pulling both of them into a hug. "Oh, it is so good to see you."

Noel hugged her tight, feeling tears press against her eyes. This was Addie. This was the woman she knew. Daughter of Lucifer or not, Addie was real, and she was theirs.

Noel didn't cry very often. In fact, she couldn't remember the last time she had. She'd learned early on that tears weren't much help if there was no one there to see them. In fact, where she'd grown up, tears only resulted in pain. But right now, she could feel them bubbling up behind her eyes.

"Why did you leave?" Micah demanded.

Addie pulled herself back and looked down at the two of them. She wiped a tear from Noel's cheek with her thumb. "I didn't want to. But I thought it would be safer for you. I thought if you were with me that Graham …" Addie cut off her words, shaking her head. "I don't know. I thought Graham might hurt you if you were with me."

"He did," Noel said softly. "He hurt Micah."

Shock splashed across Addie's face, followed by anger. "He hurt you?"

Micah squirmed under her inspection. "It's okay. I'm okay."

Addie's whole body had grown rigid. She took slow, deep breaths, as if trying to hold her anger back. "He did it. He actually hurt you."

Noel nodded slowly. "Yes. Something's wrong with him. He's not... he's not Graham anymore."

Addie nodded. "I'd hoped I was wrong. I hoped Marcus was wrong, but—"

Donovan grabbed the man at the bottom of the cliffs and pulled him away.

At the bottom of the rocks, Tess held her side, which was stained red. "I think we should probably get moving. I don't know if those raiders have any friends, but if they do, they might be heading back this way."

CHAPTER 27

ADDIE

WHILE TESS INSISTED she was fine, the pallor of her skin and the growing blood stain on her side suggested otherwise. But there was nothing to be done for it until we got back to Pitkin, so we got moving quickly.

It was hard to believe that Noel and Micah were here. After they'd climbed down from the large boulders and we were on the move, I found myself continually glancing back at them to make sure that I hadn't just imagined them. Tess and Donovan's horses had taken off all the commotion, but I had managed to snag three of the raiders' horses. The others, Donovan scattered.

The raiders that were left were curled up on the ground. Two of them were unconscious. A few rolled around in pain. Most had stumbled off. I wasn't sure what to do with them. But in the end, I let them go. After all, I wasn't an executioner.

We rode hard for the first hour. I wanted to put enough distance between ourselves and any other raiders. I was tempted to take to the sky to see if anyone was following us, but the risk was too great. Going to the air would be a giant sign of where we were. It was bad enough that the horses were leaving a trail. I had no doubt that the raiders would be able to track us eventually. But with night coming on, it should give us a little extra time.

I was also counting on the fact that the raiders were going to be a little bit scared and therefore not want to rush right back into battle with me. Plus, the sky was looking a little ominous. Hopefully a storm would break and not only erase our trail, but discourage anyone from trying to find us.

"Heads up," Donovan said, pulling me from my thoughts. I turned my head forward again. A horse headed toward us from Pitkin.

Or at least, that was what I supposed it looked like to everyone else. Torr was on the back of the horse, moving at a fast trot. I had to smile at the image. He did not look comfortable. "It's okay. It's Torr."

Noel and Micah both stared at the horse, smiles slowly crossing their faces.

I dug my heels into the side of my horse and hurried forward. Torr slowed as I approached. "Anybody hurt?" he asked.

I shook my head. "Just the bad guys. Think Vera will mind some company?"

Torr smiled. "She's already set the table."

CHAPTER 28

By the time we reached the library, the clouds had rolled in. It looked like another good storm was kicking up.

Tess walked with Torr, Noel, and Micah into the library while Donovan and I took care of the horses. I watched them disappear through the doors, not liking the paleness on Tess's face.

"Which way?" Donovan asked, holding the reins of two horses.

"This way." I led him to the old supermarket, which had been converted into a barn. Donovan walked next to me, his head on a swivel as he scanned the area.

"It's abandoned. Vera is the only one left here. You'll like her. She's gutsy."

Donovan nodded but didn't stop from watching our surroundings.

I took a breath, Donovan's wariness was making me a little wary as well. "Did you guys have any other trouble on the road?"

Donovan started to shake his head and then stopped. "The kids don't know, but two demons found us the second night. Tess and I dispatched them. But after that, there wasn't anything before the raiders. Did you have any trouble?"

I shook my head. "No. But we flew part of the way. It made it a little bit easier."

Donovan paused for a second outside the supermarket before he followed me inside. Stalls had been created out of former shelving units. Vera had four horses, three pigs, and four cows, as well as some chickens and a few goats.

The front of the supermarket was blocked by a door on rollers. But the back was partly open at the old loading dock. Beyond it was a fenced-in area where the animals could relax outside on a grassy area. Vera had even arranged for water from a water collection unit set up on the roof.

Donovan stopped still as he looked around and through the open doors to the pasture. "This is a nice little set up."

"It sure is. We can put these guys in here." I led him a few stalls down. Donovan placed one of his horses in the first one before securing the other one in the empty stall next to it. I led the other two to the stall next to it. I wasn't sure of their temperaments and didn't want to risk placing them in the same stall.

I grabbed a brush and started to wipe down one of the horses. Donovan did the same a few stalls down. Neither of us spoke, but I was okay with that. It was just nice being around someone I knew.

After we wiped the horses down, we got them some fresh water and hay before locking the barn back up for the night.

I'd appreciated the distraction the horses offered. But the whole time, I wanted to ask Donovan about Graham. At the same time, I didn't want to know. If I didn't ask, then I could pretend that everything was fine. That he was fine. Earlier up on the roof, I had seriously considered going back for answers. Now that the answers were a question away, I found myself unwilling to ask.

But the fact that Donovan and Tess were out here with Noel and Micah probably answered whatever doubts I had.

We walked along the old road approaching the library. I knew

I needed to ask him now. I didn't want to have this conversation in front of everybody. "How is he?"

Donovan didn't ask who I was talking about. He looked up at the library and then down at me. "Two days after you left, he was himself again for at least a few hours. He didn't remember anything. But then a few hours later, he was gone again." Donovan took a breath. "After you left, he threatened Noel and Micah. And Micah…"

I stopped walking. Horror, fear, and anger all surged through me. Micah and Noel had mentioned Micah getting hurt, but I hadn't had a chance to push for more details. Or I suppose I could have, but part of me didn't want to know. But I couldn't outrun the truth now. "What did he do?"

"He was trying to get Noel and Micah to tell him where you were. He placed a knife to Micah's throat," Donovan said quickly. "He cut him, just a little, but the threat for more was there."

I didn't know what to say. I didn't know what to think. I'd left Noel and Micah behind because I thought that would keep them safe. "I never should've left."

Now Donovan stopped short. "No, you did the right thing. Marcus told you what he thinks happened to Graham, right?"

I nodded.

"If Graham does anything to hurt you, he will never forgive himself. He doesn't have control right now, and until we can figure out a way to wrestle that control back, we need to keep you as far from him as possible."

I looked up into Donovan's eyes, seeing the worry there for his friend and for her. "Marcus said that if Graham sees me, he'll kill me. Or at least try to. Do you think that's true?"

Tucking some stray hairs behind his ear, Donovan sighed, looking away. "If you had asked me a week ago, I'd have said it was impossible. That Graham could never take someone's life like that, especially not yours. Now, I just don't know, Addie. As much as it kills me to say, you can't trust him. None of us can."

It a felt like the bottom had dropped out of my world. The last few days I'd had multiple fantasies of Marcus being wrong. I'd envisioned returning to Sterling Peak and everything being fine.

But they'd only been fantasies. They hadn't been real. The reality was that Graham would try to kill me if he saw me again.

And I knew in my heart that I couldn't do the same back. Whatever had happened to Graham, whatever the archangel had done to him, it was not him, not really. And Donovan was right: when Graham came back to himself and learned he'd hurt anyone, it would kill him.

Unless I killed him first.

CHAPTER 29

By the time we got back to the third floor of the library, Vera had gotten Tess settled in. She had her sitting in the bed propped up and was checking out the wound in her side.

Tess looked up when Donovan and I stepped into the doorway. She grimaced, her face looking pale. "I'll be right as rain in a few hours."

Donovan moved forward, shaking his head. "A few hours? I thought you'd be up already."

Tess glared. "Sadist."

Donovan smiled back, but I could see the worry in his eyes. The wound in her side was pretty deep. I looked around but saw no sign of Noel, Micah, or Torr.

Vera looked up and nudged her head to the left. "I had Torr take the others to the kitchen to get something to eat."

I nodded, looking back at Tess, who just waved me on. "I'm good. Go see the kids."

Heading down the hall, I worried about Tess and worried because the kids were now here with me. The whole point of me leaving was so that none of them were caught in the crosshairs. Of course, Micah had already gotten hurt, which meant I'd failed at that.

Rounding to corner, I caught sight of Noel as she paced along the back wall, glancing out the windows. "Where is she? You said the stable wasn't very far."

"It isn't," I said.

Noel stopped her pacing. Relief flashed across her face before she hurried over to me. Micah jumped to his feet and wrapped his arms around me.

I hugged them both tight, closing my eyes and just sinking into the warmth of them being here. God, I had missed them. Leaving Sterling Peak had felt like I had cut off an arm. The idea of not seeing these two had broken my heart. It felt so final. I realized that in the back of my mind, I hadn't been sure if I would ever see them again.

Micah leaned back to look up at me. "You can't leave again. We're family. We stay together."

I wanted to promise him that I wouldn't, but I couldn't make that promise. If it came down to their safety, I would leave them behind again to keep them safe.

Noel took a step back, crossing her arms over her chest. "No. I know what you're doing. Right now you're thinking you don't want to but you will if you need to. And that's not going to happen. We stay together. Micah already got hurt. You being away from us doesn't keep us from getting hurt. It just keeps you from helping us when we are."

Worry rolled through me. "Are you two okay? Graham ..." I couldn't even bring myself to say the words.

Micah's words rushed out. "I'm okay. And Marcus explained it. It wasn't him. Not really."

"It was *too* him," Noel lashed out. "It was Graham that hurt you. It wasn't anybody else. And you two need to stop thinking that Graham is anything but what he's shown us. He hurt you, Micah."

Noel's gaze speared into me. "And he'll hurt you too. I liked Graham. But you two have to stop thinking that the man we first met is in there somewhere. I don't know what's going on, but I do know that if you keep thinking that he's the old Graham, we're all going to get hurt or worse."

I wanted to argue with her. I wanted to tell her that there was a way that we would be able to get the old Graham back. But at the same time, I knew she was right. The old Graham, the one who still made my heart beat faster, was gone. And I needed to start acting like it, because Noel was right: someone was going to get hurt.

Or worse.

CHAPTER 30

EMOTIONS WERE RIDING HIGH after my talk with Noel and Micah. But Torr distracted them with the
puppies. While he took them down the hall to check them out, I headed back to see Tess. I carried a bowl of soup with me, not sure what Tess would be able to keep down.

Tess sat up in bed, her arms crossed over her chest. "I am not going to lie here like an invalid. I've gotten worse scratches in training."

"Then your training partners were trying to kill you," Vera shot back.

Donovan leaned against the wall by the door. I stepped next to him, keeping my voice low. "What's going on?"

"Vera told Tess she should rest. Tess disagrees. And I am going nowhere near that."

"Chicken," I muttered before stepping forward. "Hey, I, uh, brought you some soup."

Tess didn't take her gaze off Vera as she answered. "Take it back to the kitchen. I'll eat it there."

"You will not get out of that bed. I didn't go to all the bother of stitching you up to have you open them up." Vera stood with her hands on her hips, glaring down at her.

"Uh, how about a compromise?" I suggested. "Eat some soup, and if you're still feeling fine after that, you can get out of bed."

"Fine by me," Vera said.

"Fine, whatever," Tess replied.

Vera took the tray from me and placed it on the side table.

"You okay?" I asked Tess.

"Yeah. I just don't see what all the fuss is about. I'm fine."

Vera handed her a mug. She'd poured some soup into it. "Bottom's up."

Tess took the mug without a word and drained its contents. She handed the mug back to Vera. "See? I'm fine. Now I'm going to…" She fell forward in a dead faint.

Donovan dashed forward. "Tess!"

Vera pocketed a small glass bottle as she caught Tess and lowered her gently back onto the pillows. "Oh, she's fine. She'll sleep through the night and be the better for it."

"You drugged her?" Donovan asked.

Vera shrugged, grabbing the tray and heading for the door. "No choice. Uriels are always so stubborn."

Donovan watched Vera go, his mouth agape. "Where the heck did you find her?"

"Actually, she saved me and Torr." I gave him a brief rundown of how we met Vera and what we'd been up to since.

"That's something. She's really first generation?"

"So it seems." I reached down and pulled the blankets up over Tess and placed a hand on her forehead. She was warm but not feverishly so.

I hoped it stayed that way. I doubted that whatever weapon the raiders had used had been cleaned before it had sliced into Tess's ribs.

I shook my head. That was a problem for the future. Hopefully

Vera was right and by tomorrow morning she'd be fine. I made my way back to the kitchen with Donovan. "Where are the kids?"

Vera looked up from where she was setting the table. "Torr's still with the kids and the puppies."

"Puppies?" Donovan asked.

"He really likes those little guys. Once you guys get settled, I'll make sure that he gets one." Vera smiled at Donovan. "You're a Gabriel, aren't you?"

Donovan raised an eyebrow. "How'd you know?"

"It takes one to know one. Vera Gabriel."

I started, realizing that in all the commotion, I hadn't introduced them.

"Oh, sorry. Vera Gabriel, this is Donovan Gabriel from Sterling Peak."

Donovan took her hand. "A pleasure."

And he gave her the customary Donovan look that said she was the only woman in the world he was thinking about right at that moment.

Vera let out a cackling laugh, then patted him on the cheek. "Oh, you're a Gabriel, all right. Now I'll get this meal together while you two discuss your next steps."

I sat down across from Donovan. "Next steps. I don't know what they could possibly be. I left because I thought it would be safer for all of you if I was gone."

Donovan shook his head, letting out a heavy sigh. "I know. But I don't know if there *is* a safe right now. Graham demoted me. D'Angelo is in charge of the Seraph Force while he goes out to search for you."

"What?" I stared at him in disbelief. Graham couldn't stand D'Angelo. He was heartless, without conscience. There was no way Graham would...

Scratch that. There was no way the Graham I knew would do that. The Graham the archangel had created could do that in a heartbeat.

"How badly did he hurt Micah?" I asked softly.

Donovan winced. "It wasn't bad. I've done worse shaving, but you should've seen that poor kid's face. I still can't believe it was Graham who did it."

"He's really gone, isn't he?"

"I'm afraid so. I don't want to believe it. And sometimes I still question it, but we need to act like he's gone. We can't count on Graham returning to us."

"But how do we do that? How do we act like we don't know him?"

Donovan looked up, his gaze direct. There was no laughter in his face. This was the soldier Donovan that stared at me. "I know what the prophecy says. And I can tell you that Graham will not pull his punches. So you need to be prepared."

I pushed my chair back, as if his words and the meaning behind them would be easier to take. "You're not saying I should kill him."

"I don't want to say that. But I think you need to be prepared to do that, if it becomes necessary. Addie, I love him, but I don't recognize him right now. And I don't want to lose you just because I hope the old Graham comes back."

Rain lashed against the window, almost as if it were accentuating Donovan's point. I stared at the water as it trailed down the window frame. I wasn't ready to face Graham. Not yet. Maybe not ever.

He took a deep breath. "If you can't kill him yet, you need to at least be able to make sure he can't kill you."

CHAPTER 31

GRAHAM

T‍heir best lead had led them to a dead end. They had followed the tracks out of Sterling Peak but lost them about fifty miles east of the city. Graham wasn't sure which road to take now, but he knew he had to continue on.

The pressure inside him told him that the only priority was finding Addison.

He could feel part of him inside trying to break out from the archangel's control, but it was no use. The archangel's dictate was law. The archangel's dictate was what mattered. And the archangel's dictate was that he find Addison. By whatever means necessary.

Right now, though, he didn't know what those means could possibly be, because he had no clue as to where to look next. It had been over a week since they'd had any sign of Donovan and Tess. They still hadn't found any sign of Addison. He'd split up the search group, sending them in different directions. So now he had only Bradford and Hunter with him. They were good Rangers, well trained and disciplined.

They'd been a good choice for this mission. He hadn't worked with them before, but that didn't matter. All that mattered was that they did what needed to be done without asking questions, and both Bradford and Hunter had done that. He'd intentionally chosen them because he wasn't close to them. The people who he was close to presented too many problems. They had too many issues. They didn't understand that the archangel's order was all that mattered.

He pulled his horse to a stop as they came to an overlook on the trail. Below them was a small town. They'd come across a few in the last few days, but they hadn't provided any information.

Bradford moved his horse next to Graham's. "You want us to try down there? See if anyone's seen anything?"

Graham stared down at the town. There were a half dozen people walking about, but the town itself couldn't have more than fifty people living in it. It looked more like a stop on the way to other destinations.

But that could perhaps work in their favor. People passing through might have told stories. He nodded. "Yes. Let's see if anybody's seen our targets."

Once they arrived, Graham sent the other two Rangers to scour the town while he headed straight for the bar. He found taverns to be the place that most people congregated in these types of towns. It was also one of the places where tongues were the loosest.

He took a seat at a corner booth and ordered a beer from the waitress, who hustled over. She barely glanced at him as she placed the beer down and held out her hand. He placed two coins in it, and finally she had his attention. "Have any groups gone through lately, maybe with two teenagers?"

The waitress rolled her eyes. "There are always groups going through. You have to give me more than that."

He nodded. "What about a woman traveling on her own with long dark hair and bright blue eyes?"

"We don't get many women traveling through on their own. But we do apparently have a flying woman in the area."

Graham's head jolted up. "What did you say?"

The woman nodded her head toward the back of the bar. "Hank came in a few days ago. He's been drowning himself in his cups since then, ranting about some flying woman. He keeps saying that the angels have returned."

Graham looked in the direction the waitress indicated. All he could make out was a man in a dusty brown shirt with darker pants, leaning over the table, his hair obscuring his face.

"Hank never was all there to begin with, but whatever happened out there really shook him. You need anything else?"

Graham shook his head. "No, not right now."

The waitress quickly made her exit. Graham picked up his glass and headed for the man at the back table.

Hank leaned heavily on the table in front of him, his head propped up on his right hand. The other one held the handle of his beer mug, although he made no move to drink. From the half-mast of his eyes, he'd obviously been drinking more than his fair share in the recent past. The man continuously mumbled to himself.

A few people were giving him curious, wary glances. But no one made any moves toward him.

Graham placed his beer on the table. It took a few seconds for Hank to notice he was there. He looked up, his head nearly falling back as he blinked up at Graham.

"Mind if I join you?" Graham asked, already sliding into the chair across from him.

"Sure. Whatever," Hank mumbled.

Graham placed his own hands around his mug. "I hear you ran into a flying woman."

Hank's eyes went wide, his head snapping back up. "She was real."

Graham nodded. "I have no doubt. I've seen her too."

Hank's mouth fell open, and then he shimmied his chair closer to Graham. The stench of body odor, dried sweat, and unwashed hair wafted toward Graham, mixed with bad breath.

"She took out my group. She just flew right in and yanked people off their horses. I ain't never seen anything like that. It's the Angel War all over again."

"Where exactly did you see this woman?"

Hank waved generally toward the door. "Out there. I'm not going back out there, maybe not ever. It's not safe." His chin dropped down and his eyes closed.

Graham kicked the table.

Hank's eyes shot open once again, blinking repeatedly.

"*Where* exactly out there did you see them?"

"By the dry riverbed. We were coming down on a group. Just going to ask them for a few things." Hank mumbled.

"Who was in this group?"

Hank shrugged. "Big guy, girl, two kids."

Graham's heart began to beat faster. "And you said this happened by the dry riverbed?"

Hank nodded and jerked his head back up. He'd nearly fallen asleep. "Yup. I'm never going back out there. Never."

Graham stood. *Well, I certainly am.*

After speaking with the waitress again, Graham got directions to the dry riverbed. It was a thirty-minute ride from the town. The waitress explained there wasn't much out that way except for an old, abandoned town another ninety minutes beyond it.

It took them closer to an hour to find the bed. What was clear to see was that there had been a fight here. There were even a few men still laying dead on the ground where they had fallen.

He narrowed his eyes, picturing Addison during the fight with the demon horde. She had rushed in to protect him and Donovan. Then she had rushed back again to protect Torr. That was after racing ahead of everyone else in Sterling Peak to protect the people of Blue Forks.

If it was Donovan and the others who had been chased by the raiders, Addie coming to their rescue was no surprise.

It was, however, a foolish mistake. She had left Sterling Peak to keep the ones she cared about from getting hurt. But as soon as she had seen them in danger, she had flown right in. He wondered, though, if Addison had been keeping an eye on them ever since they left Sterling Peak. Had she been close the whole time?

Or was it just a twist of fate that allowed her to arrive at the right time?

But he knew in his gut it wasn't either. It wasn't a twist of fate or her keeping an eye on them. It was destiny. He and Addison would fight, and the world would change. It was destiny that brought her to this moment, and him as well. It was destiny that led him to that small town, and that had pointed him in this direction. Addison was running, trying to escape something that had been preordained hundreds of years ago.

But there was no stopping it. She had merely postponed the inevitable.

He stood up. "We're heading that way."

"Are you sure it's them?" Bradford asked.

Graham smiled. "Oh, it's them all right. Let's go."

CHAPTER 32

NOEL

THE LAST FEW days had been surreal. After being constantly on the go, stopping was a complete reality shift. And then there was seeing Addie again. That first night, Addie had curled up with her and Micah, telling them about her and Torr's trip. As much as she wanted to hear it, Noel had fallen asleep only a few minutes into the telling. She slept straight through to noon the next day without a single dream.

Then the next few days had been spent reading books, playing with puppies, getting to know Vera—who was one seriously cool lady—and generally acting like the previous week hadn't happened.

But it had, and until she saw Addie, Noel hadn't realized just how angry she was at her. She was happy to see her too. Seeing her here had made her realize just how scared she'd been that she never would see her again.

Which led her back to the anger. Because there was no avoiding one simple fact: Addie had left them. Noel knew that Addie thought she was doing it for their own good, but the truth was she had *left* them. And Noel wasn't quite ready to forgive her for that.

The sun was just setting on the horizon as Noel took a seat in the lean-to on the roof. She had to admit that Vera had a pretty nice setup here. High ground to see if anyone was coming in. Gardens set up in the middle of the library so that it was protected and also so that no one would be able to see it from outside or even suspect it was there.

She had a stable full of farm animals. And every book she could possibly want to read.

The one downfall was that she was on her own, but overall, Vera didn't seem to mind that.

Noel wished that when she and Micah had been on the run, they'd been able to find a setup half as good as Vera's. They never had. It seemed like their stomachs had been constantly empty and the roofs they found themselves under were always leaking. It wasn't until they had linked up with Addie that their lives had actually taken a turn for the better.

And then Addie had walked away from them.

Noel was trying to get rid of her anger. Micah wasn't mad at Addie. He didn't even seem to be angry at Graham.

How was that possible? She was so angry at that guy that she could practically spit.

She understood why Addie was having trouble accepting her role in all of this. Noel had seen that look on her face when she watched Graham. She'd seen that same look on Graham's face when he looked at Addie, before that stupid angel had come along.

But he was no longer that Graham. And Addie really needed to accept that if they were going to make it through this.

The hatch to the roof opened. Noel wasn't surprised when Addie stepped through and crossed the roof toward her. "We're almost set. Vera is insisting on giving us a big breakfast before we leave tomorrow."

"That's nice," Noel said. "She's nice."

"She is."

"How's Tess?"

"Still not great. We'll have to take it slow to make sure that she doesn't reopen her stitches. Vera wants us to stay another few days, but I feel like we need to get going." Addie took a deep breath. "And I feel like you're still mad at me."

Noel shrugged, not looking at her.

Addie crouched down next to her chair. She took Noel's hand. "I'm sorry, Noel. I thought I was doing what was best for you and Micah. I thought that by leaving you behind, I was keeping you safe. I thought you would be better off without me."

"We've never been better off without you." Tears pressed against the back of Noel's eyes, but she refused to let them fall. "You know how awful our life was before we met you. No matter what happens, our life, our lives are better when we're with you. But you didn't even ask us. Before you, no one thought we were important, Addie. No one."

"But that wasn't true in Sterling Peak," Addie said. "Donovan, Tess, Marcus: you two are important to all of them."

"It's not the same. They're not ..." She shook her head.

Addie squeezed her hand. "Not family."

Noel nodded, her mouth tight.

"I'm sorry, Noel. I really, really am." She took a deep breath. "But I promise you, from this point forward, we stay together."

Noel looked over at her. "Do you mean it?"

Addie nodded. "I can't promise that I won't try to keep you safe. But I can promise I won't run away again, not like that."

Noel reached over and grabbed her, hugging her tight. "Promise?"

Addie wrapped her arms around her. "I promise, Noel. Together."

A shudder ran through Noel, this one filled with relief. They stayed together for a while before Noel finally pulled away, feeling more than a little embarrassed. She wasn't big on emotional displays. She stood up, and Addie did the same. Noel nodded toward the middle stand at the edge of the roof. "What's that, by the way?"

"Oh, that's Vera's telescope."

Noel had heard of telescopes, but she'd never actually seen one. "You think Vera would mind if I looked through it?"

Addie grinned, pulling her toward it. "I think she'd mind if you didn't. Come on."

Addie showed her where to look through as well as how to adjust it and move it around. She said that you weren't really supposed to move it around, but Vera used it as more of a spyglass to see what was going on in the area.

Noel peered through the telescope and let out a gasp. She pulled back, looking at the town below them. Everything seemed so close. She knew that was what a telescope did, but it was something altogether different actually seeing it. She leaned back down again, scanning the area. This was really cool.

A dark spot appeared in the distance, pulling her attention. "How do I zoom in on this thing?"

Addie tapped a round knob on the right of the telescope. "Just turn this to zoom in or out."

Noel nodded, leaning back down again, turning the knob.

The image came into view. It was a horse. There was a man on its back. She didn't recognize him, but something about the way he sat in the saddle seemed familiar. She glanced to the side of the man and realized that there were two more. She didn't recognize the one in the middle, but her heart lodged in her throat as she zoomed in on the third man.

"Noel?"

Noel stepped back from the telescope. Her mouth fell open. Her heart began to pound. "It's Graham. He's found us."

CHAPTER 33

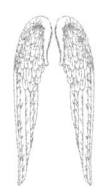

GRAHAM

A FLASH of light at the top of the tall building in the distance pulled Graham's attention. He paused, but the flash didn't repeat. He spurred his horse to move faster, his anticipation building.

But as Graham approached the town of Pitkin, it looked completely abandoned. Most of the buildings were on the edge of collapse. Graham's hopes began to dim that this might be the end of his quest.

The trail definitely led to the abandoned town, but it was entirely possible that they'd simply passed through it and moved on. They could have taken shelter for the night and moved on at first light.

It was entirely possible that Addison was days ahead of him. *I should've moved faster.*

The push in his chest to find Addison had only grown stronger in the last few hours.

As he reached the edge of the town, he nodded to Bradford and Hunter to split off and search. Graham himself took the main street. He stayed on the back of his horse but moved slowly down the old road, scanning the area for any movement while always keeping the building at the end of the street in his sights. That was the building he'd seen a flash from when they'd been a few hundred yards from the town's edge. It only appeared once, but once had been enough. Something had made that flash.

As he made his way down the street, though, he saw no signs of life. No footprints. He definitely saw no signs that anyone was living here.

Then he heard the moo of a cow. He pulled on his reins, and his horse came to a stop. He tilted his head, listening. The moo came again.

He turned his horse to the right. An old supermarket sat there. He led his horse down the alley next to it. Around the back, a pasture had been created and fully fenced in. A cow snacked on some grass while a pig sat in some mud that had been created by last night's storm. Chickens and a few goats scampered around as well. A glance inside through the loading dock doors showed a very organized barn.

He smiled. Somebody was definitely living here. And he was betting that they had at least seen Addison.

Bradford came up from behind him. "What on earth is this?"

"Proof that someone's still around. Have you seen anything else?"

Bradford shook his head. "Besides this, the place looks abandoned."

"The building at the end of the street. That's where we'll search."

"Did you see something?"

Graham nodded. "Yes. And hopefully it means all of our targets are together."

CHAPTER 34

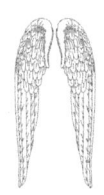

ADDIE

THROUGH THE TELESCOPE, I could see Graham as he approached the edge of town. And despite what I knew, despite everything that had happened, my heart still quickened at the sight of him. But I quickly squashed the feeling down. It was not my Graham who approached.

I needed to prepare. I might not be ready to kill him, but I also wasn't ready to have him try and kill me, or anyone I cared about. Grabbing Noel's hand, I pulled her toward the stairs. "We need to warn the others."

Side by side, we raced down the stairs. Donovan came running down the hall, hearing our rapid approach. "What's wrong?"

"Graham. He just rode into town," I said, pleased my voice came out even.

Donovan swore softly. "What do we do?"

Vera had appeared in the hallway behind Donovan, stepping out of Tess's room, a concerned look on her face.

"We need to get out of here now," I said.

Vera shook her head. "I'm afraid your friend can't move

quickly just yet. Her stitches reopened. I had to restitch them. If you put her on a horse right now ..." Vera shook her head.

"Dammit."

Torr appeared from the kitchen, Noel and Micah with him.

"We need to go. You can't let Graham get you," Micah said, his voice shaking.

I knew he was right. But I also knew we wouldn't be able to move fast enough as a group to outrun him. And I certainly couldn't leave them behind to face Graham without me.

I took a deep breath and then stared at each of the people in front of me one by one. "I guess it's time. I have to face him."

CHAPTER 35

GRAHAM

Graham wasn't sure what to expect in the old building, which turned out to be a library.

Addison certainly hadn't had time to create a herd of animals. She hadn't been here long enough. Which meant that there were other people in the town. Knowing Addie, she had befriended them and not taken them over. So it was possible the people would fight with her.

Which meant that they would die with her as well. It was unfortunate, but there was no help for it. If Addie would just hand herself over, no one else had to die. But that wasn't her way.

She would fight, even though it was useless. The archangel was on Graham's side. And his will would be done.

Bradford and Hunter flanked Graham as he approached the front door of the library. He nodded at Bradford, who swung the door open and slipped inside. An arrow pierced his chest as he fell back.

Graham grabbed him and pulled him out of the way as he slipped inside. Then he rolled to the right, taking cover behind an old table as arrows rained down on its top. He smiled. "Is that you, Donovan?"

"It sure is." Donovan's voice was hard.

Perfect. Donovan was an intimidating soldier, but he didn't have a lust for the kill. His emotions would make him weak.

Graham shifted his tone. "Are you okay?"

There was a hesitation before Donovan answered. "Why would you care?"

Answering that question was easy. He knew Donovan hoped that Graham would return. "It's me, Donovan. I just want to help. It's actually me."

Once again, Donovan hesitated. "Graham?"

Graham peeked above the table. "Hey. Don't shoot me, okay?"

Underneath the table, out of Donovan's view, he pulled a throwing knife and kept it tucked in his hand. "It's me again. I just want to make sure you guys are all okay."

"We're fine," Donovan said.

"Good, good. I got worried when I heard about the raiders. I thought maybe you were in trouble. Was anybody hurt?"

This time there was another hesitation from Donovan. "No, no one."

"Good, that's good. And Addie? Is she okay?"

The shuffling of feet gave away Donovan's position. He was poised behind a bookcase. Graham tried not to smile. Donovan's restlessness was always a problem. Without warning, Graham rolled to his right, coming up into a crouch, and let the knife go.

CHAPTER 36

ADDIE

Donovan stood by the bookcase thirty feet away from me. I was on the other side of the foyer, ducked down behind the old wooden circulation desk.

I glanced around the corner. Graham was crouched behind an upended table. I listened to Graham's voice as he spoke to Donovan. His words sounded good; they sounded right.

But the tone was all wrong. There was no emotion in his words. It was as if he were reading a script, and badly at that.

I prayed that Donovan could tell the difference as well.

Without warning, Graham rolled to the side and let loose with a knife.

But Donovan was prepared. He rolled out of the way just as one of the other men barreled in the door. I was so focused on Graham, I hadn't noticed the door springing open.

The man let loose with arrow after arrow, aiming at Donovan's location. Donovan was backed up against the wall.

I bolted from my spot, my wings flying open.

The man's eyes grew large for a second before I slammed into him, lifting him up and tucking my head as we crashed through the glass door behind him. I tossed him to the side, and he slammed into an old fence, breaking through and laying on the ground. A small object hurtled toward me as I whirled around. Caught by surprise, I didn't have time to move before the knife embedded in my side. I let out a cry as Graham stepped through the broken glass, chucking knife after knife.

Bolting into the air, I travelled just far enough to get out of Graham's range, and then dove for the roof of a partially collapsed building. Pain lanced through my side. I touched down, pain trembling through me with every step.

I reached down with shaky fingers and pulled the knife out, swallowing down the cry as I yanked more tissue with it. Blood poured from the wound.

I grabbed the handkerchief from around my neck and pressed it against my side, breathing slowly through my teeth. I unlinked my belt with one hand. I had to release the bandage long enough to bring the belt up to cover the wound and keep bandage in place. It was a sad sort of first-aid attempt, but it was all I could do at the moment.

From my perch, I glanced over and noticed that the man I had thrown had disappeared from his spot. I grimaced. I hadn't wanted to kill him, but I wouldn't have minded if he was hurt bad enough to be out of the fight.

I crouched down low, not sure where Graham was either. The third soldier still lay on the ground in front of the library.

An arrow shot over my head.

I threw myself down. Spots burst in front of my eyes as I jarred my injury. I gritted my teeth as pain vibrated through me.

I army-crawled backward as running feet thundered toward my location. More than anything, I wanted to take off into the air, but I knew with my injury that in all likelihood, I'd be too slow to avoid an arrow in the back.

And that arrow would be shot by Graham. That floored me.

The injury in my side was thanks to him as well. He was actually trying to kill me. Marcus had been right.

I reached the edge of the roof line and lowered myself over, quickly dropping to the ground to avoid stretching out my torso and aggravating my wound. But the pain when I touched down still left me feeling a little light-headed.

I was right next to the supermarket. I dashed over and unlocked the back gate. A few horses grazed in the pasture and moved to the back gate at my approach. An arrow whistled through the air. I bolted through the gate, slamming into the side of one of the animals. The horse let out a whinny before it tore out of the pasture. Two others followed. Ignoring the pain, I used them for cover and spread my wings, flying along the side of them. Graham let out a scream of rage.

The horses galloped back around toward the library. By a copse of tall old trees, I slipped away from them and knelt on the ground for a moment, catching my breath. My side felt like it was on fire. Spots danced at the edge of my vision. As quickly as I could manage, I scrambled up one of the trees, half climbing, half-flying. Each movement was agony.

Focused on the horses, Graham sprinted around the side of the supermarket, heading toward the library. I grimaced as I used my wings to silently move myself away from the trunk. I perched up high, staying quiet and still.

It's time, Addie. It's you or him.

The words raged through my mind. I knew they were right. But could I do it? Could I hurt or even kill Graham?

Noel was right. He'd already hurt Micah. And he'd just tried to kill Donovan. I didn't know if the archangel's effect was permanent, but I did know that Graham was playing for keeps. The slash in my side was proof of that. We were lucky no one had been killed yet. He wasn't pulling punches.

Which meant I couldn't either.

Graham slowed as he reached the group of trees. Hidden by

the foliage, he couldn't see me. Not that he looked up. He was still scanning closer to the ground. He slowed as he approached my spot on the ground.

I waited, knowing it was now or never. Graham was going to kill me. I needed to defend myself. I needed to defend everyone in the library.

I stepped off the ledge and plunged down. At the last second, Graham looked up. I was moving too fast for him to get an arrow off. I slammed into his chest. He crashed to the ground, but not before the arrow gripped in his hand pierced my left wing.

Screaming in pain and agony, my fist swung and connected with his face. He grunted, going for my throat. I slammed my knee into his balls. He curled up as I slammed an uppercut into his chin. His eyes rolled back, and he went limp.

I stumbled off of him, my chest heaving as I crashed to my knees. My vision blurred, darkening at the edges.

"Addie!" Donovan yelled from somewhere to my right.

"Over here," I called out, crawling back from Graham's quiet form. He was breathing, but I knew that some of his ribs, if not his clavicle, were broken. He wouldn't be rushing after us anytime soon.

And neither would I. Each breath was painful. The black at the edge of my vision only grew larger. I was nauseated, light-headed, and drowning in pain all at the same time.

Donovan came to a halt staring down at Graham's prone form. "Is he …"

"Still breathing." I looked up at Donovan. "I can't kill him."

Donovan nodded. "I understand. But that means we need to move, and we need to move quickly."

I struggled slowly to my feet, the world swaying.

Donovan gasped as he darted forward to grip my arm and help me stand. "You're hurt."

"Yeah. And I think it's bad." The world darkened, and I fell into Donovan's arms.

CHAPTER 37

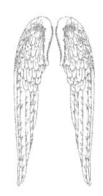

It felt like my left wing was on fire. When I came to, I lay on the ground. Blood seeped from the wound in my left wing. It mixed with the blood from the wound in my side. God, I was a mess.

And alone.

I frowned. Had Donovan left me?

I got to my knees, then kneeled on the ground, taking shallow breaths, not wanting to take anything deeper and trying not to whimper.

"Addie," Donovan said softly from behind my head.

I struggled to look back at him. He flicked a gaze at me but then directed his attention back to the ground. And I realized why.

Graham's eyes were open. Then they closed again. Like me, Graham was obviously in no shape to fight. I watched Donovan from the corner of my eye, wondering if he could do what I couldn't. Could he actually take Graham's life?

But he simply stared down at his friend, then walked over to me. "Can you walk?"

I nodded and held up a hand. "With a little help."

Donovan gently took my hand and helped me up. I blew through my teeth as the movement jarred both injuries.

Donovan winced. "Sorry."

I looked back at Graham. "What are we going to do about him?"

Torr appeared as if out of thin air. "I'll keep an eye on him."

Donovan, world-renowned warrior, cursed as he jumped. "Torr, don't sneak up on us like that."

Torr rolled his eyes, a smirk on his face. "Get going. Her wound looks bad."

I forced him to meet my gaze. "You won't kill him, will you?"

Torr stared back at me for the longest time and finally shook his head. "He's injured. He's not a threat right now, even though we all know he's going to be a threat again as soon as he heals. But no, I won't hurt him. I won't help him either, though."

I nodded, knowing that was as good a reassurance as I was going to get. And I wasn't really sure what to do about Graham. Because Torr was right. As soon as he healed, he would be a threat to us again. But I couldn't just kill him. And I couldn't imagine either Donovan, Tess, or Torr could bring themselves to do that either.

Donovan tugged on my arm gently. "Let's go get you looked at first, and then we'll figure out what to do with him, okay?"

It was the right call. The pain right now was throbbing in my side, and I didn't even want to think about retracting my wings with that injury. So with one last look at Graham, I let Donovan lead me away, wondering if I would be able to figure out an answer to the question of what to do with him.

CHAPTER 38

GRAHAM

THE VOICES INTRUDED on the darkness that swirled around Graham. It took a moment for him to recognize them. Donovan and Addie. He'd found Addie. His heart leapt at the idea of seeing her. But then images crashed through his mind. He saw himself hurting Addie.

He cringed away from the violence. How could he have done that? How could he have hurt her?

A third voice joined the other two, and it took him a moment to place it. Torr. So he'd gone with Addie. That was good. Torr was a strong, capable fighter. And he was loyal to Addie.

Graham was having trouble focusing on the conversation. He felt like he was kind of shifting in and out of consciousness. It seemed like they didn't know what to do with him. Finally, the voices went silent. He cracked his eyes open.

Torr sat crouched next to him. His voice was cold, hard. "I knew you were awake."

Graham looked up into his face. This close, he could see the humanity underneath the demon exterior. He really did look young. But he hoped he wasn't. Because he had something to ask him. And it was not something he wanted to ask a child. Graham licked his lips. "I need you to do something for me."

Torr scoffed. "Why would I do anything for you?"

"You're going to want to do this."

"Why? What is it?"

Graham took a deep breath, ignoring the pain that rattled through him. "I need you to kill me."

CHAPTER 39

ADDIE

With Donovan's help, I managed to get back to the library. But I completely balked at the idea of going back up those stairs. He sat me down, leaning me against the old circulation desk. "I'll go get some supplies. Don't go anywhere."

I gave him a small smile. "Ha-ha, no danger of that."

He squeezed my arm and then ran for the stairs.

I closed my eyes, letting my head fall back. Graham had tried to kill me. This whole time I'd been telling myself that I had been wrong, that Marcus had once again misinterpreted the prophecy. I pictured Graham as he had been back in his home. The light on his face, the smile. He been a perfect gentleman, perfect host. He'd been a friend and more.

And now he'd tried to kill me. If I had fallen a few inches to the right or left, or if he had taken a step in either direction, that arrow would've gone right through my chest. I was lucky. There were no two ways about it.

I was lucky, and he was deadly. This was what it had actually come to. And if we didn't kill him now, he would heal, and he would come after me again.

But I couldn't do it. If I couldn't kill him in the heat of battle, I certainly couldn't kill him when he was injured.

So what was I going to do?

Footsteps on the stairs caused me to open my eyes. Noel and Micah rushed toward me, their eyes wide. Noel's steps faltered when she caught sight of me, but Micah rushed to my side, dropping down to the ground. "Addie."

I gave him a small smile. "It's okay. I'll be okay."

Micah's eyes filled with tears. "Did Graham do this to you?"

I wanted to tell him no. I wanted to tell him that if Graham was in his right mind, he would never do something like this. But I also knew I couldn't lie to him about the danger that Graham posed. "Yes," I said softly, "it was Graham."

Noel dropped down to my other side. "I knew it. We never should've trusted him. We never should have left Blue Forks."

My head swam, but I knew this conversation needed to happen. "Hey, he helped us in Blue Forks. I don't know if we'll ever get that Graham back, but something was done to him. This is not who he is. He's being made to act this way. The Graham that helped us, the Graham that we know, that Graham was a good man. This one is ... is ..." I struggled, looking for a word that would fit.

"A monster," Micah said.

I agreed softly. "Yes, he is."

Donovan hurried down the stairs. Right behind him was Vera with first-aid supplies. "I need a little room, you two."

Micah and Noel backed away but stayed close.

Vera took Micah's place, tsking as she inspected all of the wounds. "Well, you got yourself in a fine state."

I grimaced. "You know me, always throwing myself into one horrible situation after the next."

Vera arched an eyebrow. "Let's see what's going on here."

I felt Micah and Noel's gazes on me, so I tried to keep my face as blank as possible while Vera inspected my wounds. But when she touched my wing, it felt like she'd tried to rip it off. I cried out.

Vera backed up immediately, putting her hands up. "Sorry, sorry." She dug through her box of first-aid supplies and pulled out a bottle. "This will kill the pain, but it will also knock you out. Are you okay with that? I think it would be better for you when I work on you if you weren't awake for it."

I looked at the little bottle. Not being conscious for a little while sounded kind of like heaven. I wouldn't have to think about Graham. I wouldn't what I think about our next steps. And I wouldn't be in pain.

"I'm okay with that."

Vera nodded. "I thought you might be."

CHAPTER 40

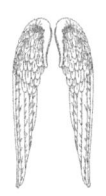

GRAHAM

THE YOUNG DEMON sat crouched next to Graham, surprise flashing across his face. "You want me to kill you?"

Graham nodded and then winced at the movement. "I don't know how long I have. I come in and out of consciousness. It's like someone else moves into my body and takes over. I think he's gone now because I'm hurt. You were right. As soon as I feel better, I will go after Addie again. I will try to kill her again. You need to kill me now before I can do that. Please, Torr. I know what I'm asking, and I also know how much you love Addie. This is the only way to guarantee her safety."

Torr took a step back, shaking his head. "I ... I can't do that."

Graham wanted to grab him and shake some sense into him. All he managed to do was sit up. He nearly passed out with the effort. He looked around. His knife had slipped from his sheath and now lay ten feet away from him. "Just give me my knife. I'll do it."

Torr turned to the knife. Graham knew he was thinking about it. Graham stayed silent, letting Torr go through his mental gymnastics, trying to figure out the right thing to do. Torr was a smart kid. He knew what the right thing to do for his family was. He'd realize Graham was too great a risk. He'd realize the only way to protect his family was to get rid of him.

Graham could admit he was a little worried about whether or not he'd have the strength to kill himself. Even the idea of it was the antithesis of everything he believed about the sanctity of life. But he knew he would hurt and kill to get to Addie. The world would be safer without him in it. And protecting others was very much who he was.

But even if he could mentally prepare himself for the task, he wasn't sure he could physically do it. His arm wasn't feeling that great. He wasn't sure he'd have the strength to do the deed before the angel took over. But it was entirely possible that if Torr just left him be, he would die anyway, especially exposed out here.

Graham studied Torr as he looked between the knife and him. There was a strange sort of shimmer over him. Was that his injury affecting his vision?

But then he realized it was actually his invisibility. Torr had let Graham see him.

From the corner of his eye, Graham noticed movement. Before he could fully turn his head, an arrow lodged in Graham's chest, and he fell back with a cry. Torr's eyes went wide, and then he was a blur of motion.

Graham turned his head, watching as Bradford moved toward him. He held his bow in his hands. He pulled another arrow and notched it, taking his time. He was ten feet away when he stopped. "D'Angelo sends his regards."

He pulled the string back. Torr tackled him from the side. The arrow dropped to the ground. Bradford cried out, no doubt because he had no idea what had just hit him.

Torr landed on top of him. But then he scrambled off him almost as soon as he got him to the ground, a look of horror on his face. Blood began to seep from a wound on Bradford's head. He'd hit a large rock and lay there limply. Was he dead?

Torr backed away, shaking his head. "I didn't mean to."

Graham wanted to tell him it was okay. He wanted to tell him that it wasn't his fault. But he couldn't say anything as the pain in his chest increased. His breathing became difficult. Graham tried to keep his eyes open, but it was a battle he wasn't going to win. He closed his eyes and prayed that he didn't open them again.

CHAPTER 41

ADDIE

THE NEXT FEW days were a blur. I could only remember flashes of time. I remember being loaded into the wagon and the jostling of it as it started to move. I lay on my stomach because my wings were still out. Noel crouched down next to me. "It's going to be okay, Addie. You just sleep."

I took her advice and closed my eyes.

The next time I opened them, the wagon was still moving. I lay on a bed of blankets. I vaguely remembered snippets of time in between but nothing concrete. Micah sat in the corner of the wagon bed as it moved, trying to read a book. How was he managing that with all the movement?

A quick glance showed Noel and Torr asleep in opposite corners of the wagon. Through the hole at the end of the wagon, I could see Tess and Donovan sitting up front.

Micah made his way over to me. "You're awake," he said in an excited whisper.

My head felt fuzzy, but I sat up slowly, gingerly waiting for the pain in my wings to explode across my back. There was only a slight twinge.

Micah nodded toward my wing. "It's healed really fast. You can barely even see the injury now. The feathers are starting to come back too."

It did feel much better. With a tentative move, I started to retract my wings. It didn't feel horrible, so I continued with a wince, ready to stop the minute pain lashed through me. I managed to retract them completely. I slumped in relief. Thank God. I was worried that I would have to keep them out forever. It wouldn't exactly have been easy to slip in and out of places with my wings out.

I kept my voice low so as not to wake the other two. "Where are we going?"

"To New Chicago. Tess's family is there. We're going to stay there while we figure out what to do."

"How long have we been traveling?"

"Five days. You've been really out of it."

I could imagine. Even now, my thoughts felt sluggish.

Micah scrambled over to the side of the wagon, grabbed a canteen, and brought it back. "Here. Vera said that you'd be thirsty when you finally woke up."

Vera was right. I grabbed the canteen gratefully and took a long drink. My mouth felt dry, my teeth felt fuzzy, and the water felt so good. I let out a little sigh. "Thanks, Micah. Is everyone else okay?"

He nodded. "We haven't had any problems. We haven't run into any demons. We stayed away from all towns. With your wings out, we didn't want to risk anyone seeing them. Vera gave us this wagon and the horses to use, plus a bunch of food. That was pretty cool of her, wasn't it?"

I smiled. "Yes, it was. She's a pretty cool lady."

"Do you think we'll see her again?"

"I don't know. I hope so."

"I hope she's okay," Micah said.

"I'm sure she will be. She's a strong lady. And she's been on her own for a long time."

"But see that's the thing, she's not on her own. Not anymore."

I found myself unable to parse what Micah was saying. "What do you mean?"

Micah bit his lip, then dropped his voice, leaning forward. "Vera is taking care of Graham."

CHAPTER 42

GRAHAM

There was movement in Graham's room. He could tell someone was moving around, and they weren't being subtle about it. But he was having trouble getting his eyelids to open. His thoughts were muddled. He felt pressure, as if someone was leaning on the bed. He tensed, waiting for the attack.

Someone licked his hand.

His eyes flew open. He looked into the pale eyes of a reddish-brown dog with a wide face. The dog licked his cheek and then hopped off the bed. Graham stared at it, wondering if he was going crazy.

"*Finally.* You're awake."

Graham turned his head. An older women sat in the chair next to his bed, knitting, of all things. She placed her needles and wool aside and walked over to the bed. She placed her hand on his forehead and nodded. "Your fever broke sometime last night. It was touch and go for a while. Your color's a little better now too."

Graham stared up at her. "Who are you?"

"I am Vera Gabriel, and you are Graham Michael."

Graham looked around, trying to figure out where he was, but it was just a basic room. Through the window, all he could see was sky. "Where am I?"

"Oh, I'll explain all that in a minute. Right now we need to get some food into you. I'll be right back."

She disappeared out the door, and the dog followed her. Three small puppies appeared at the door and scampered around the room. Graham stared at them, wondering if they were real or if he was hallucinating. He closed his eyes and drifted off.

Vera's voice cut into his sleep. "No more of that. You need to get some food in you."

His eyes opened slowly. He looked to the ground, but he didn't see any of the puppies. It must have been a hallucination. The dog wasn't there either.

Vera placed a tray with a bowl on it on the table next to the bed. She leaned down. "Okay, let's get you sitting up."

It was a struggle to do more than raise his head. He felt so weak.

Vera did not have the same issue. With surprising strength, she pulled him up into a sitting position with a very practiced and efficient movement.

Graham's eyes nearly popped out of his head. "You're awfully strong."

She winked at him. "All the boys say so. Now, have some soup."

Graham tried to reach for the bowl, but Vera shook her head. "I don't think you're quite ready for that yet. Let me."

She picked up the bowl and then started to feed him. It was some sort of chicken soup filled with vegetables. It was delicious. At the same time, Graham couldn't believe he was being spoon-fed by this woman. What exactly was going on?

He finished about half the bowl before his stomach was filled. He put up a hand.

Vera nodded, putting the rest of the bowl on the side table. "You haven't really eaten much the last few days. But it's good to get at least a little something in you. You'll be feeling pretty weak until you get your strength back up again."

The food had revived him a little bit and also brought on his curiosity. "Where am I?"

Vera pulled the chair closer to the side of the bed, and then she popped her feet up on the edge of it. "What do you remember?"

Graham paused, trying to sort through the large holes in his memories. He didn't remember anything immediately before waking up, and before that it was only snatches of memory. Had he seen Addie? And there was something about Donovan.

He gasped, remembering Addie landing on him as he shot an arrow through her wing. "Oh my God. Addie."

Vera nodded. "You brought two guys here to kill her. Your two comrades didn't make it, by the way. I buried them out back."

"Is she okay? Is she alive?"

"She is. She's hurt pretty badly. But she'll heal. Just like you."

Graham closed his eyes, shame rolling over him. "You should've let me die."

"I don't think the archangel Michael would happy if I'd done that. Besides, he'd just go find someone else to go after Addie."

Graham's eyes opened. "You know about the archangel?"

"Addie and Donovan gave me the rundown. You have some good friends there."

"They should have finished me off."

"You were injured, and they couldn't bring themselves to do it."

"They should have. As soon as I'm better, I have no doubt I'll be back to that monster that I was and track her down again."

"Maybe," Vera mused. "Maybe not. But right now, I think you should sleep. That's the only way you're going to heal."

Part of Graham didn't want to heal. But it was like the suggestion had some sort of hypnotic effect, because he already felt his eyes closing. "Thank you." The words slipped out of his mouth, years of politeness ingrained in him.

"You are very welcome, Graham."

CHAPTER 43

ADDIE

NEW CHICAGO WAS NOT the city I had seen in books. It was largely abandoned, as were most of the former major cities. After the wars, disease had run rampant. People who stayed in them often died in them. It was decades before the cities had been cleaned out enough to be even partially used again. Still, the memory of all those that had passed remained, and people didn't want to make the cities their home. Many of the buildings were left abandoned, especially the tall skyscrapers, as most of them still held the bodies of their previous owners.

When people talked about Chicago now, they were talking about the smaller communities around New Chicago that had been built.

Tess's extended family was part of one of them. The Uriels here were incredibly wealthy, which was both a blessing and a curse. A blessing because it meant that they had lots of properties from which to choose to hide out in. A curse because it also meant that they were well-connected and well-known.

I was glad to see Tess had healed pretty well from her own injury. She led us to a small manor house on the outskirts of a large village. The house was a mile away from the next one, nicely isolated. Even so, we arrived at dusk, intentionally, hoping that no one would see us.

The house itself was smaller than any house up on Sterling Peak by a large margin. But I liked the look of it. Two stories tall, it was a perfectly square pale yellow house with gray-blue shutters.

Tess opened the door and ushered us all in. "I'm afraid we'll have to keep the candles off for now. I don't want to let anyone know we're here. If word gets out, they're going to assume at the very least that Donovan and the kids are here. But someone will figure out that you're here too. So at night, we'll have to stay dark."

The front entry held a wide hall with a large staircase to the left of it. On the left-hand side was a large sitting room, and on the right-hand side was a dining room that opened into a kitchen. The stone fireplace was five feet wide and four feet tall. It could have fit a dining room table.

Micah's mouth dropped open as he looked at it. "That's a fireplace?"

Tess smiled. "Back in the day, they used to cook all their meals in it. So it's a fireplace, a stove, and a way to heat the whole house. This house dates back to well before the Angel War. It's been in my family for generations. No one comes here anymore. It's got running water, but it doesn't have any electricity, which in my family means that people will be roughing it if they stayed here. But I've always kept it cleaned and stocked. I like it. It's comfortable and not fussy."

Which meant it was just like Tess. Tess had uprooted her life to protect Noel and Micah. She had been injured and hadn't offered one iota of complaint. The house was strong and sturdy and would stand the test of time, just like she would. Gratitude overwhelmed me. "Thanks, Tess. For everything."

Tess smiled back at me. "Anytime. Now, I don't know about you guys, but I definitely could use some sleep in a real bed. And a shower. So let me show you guys where everybody can crash."

Upstairs, there were four bedrooms. Noel and I would share one. Micah and Torr were shown to another one, and then Donovan and Tess each got their own rooms.

Tess tried to give me her room, saying she had no problem bunking with Noel, but I wanted to stay near Noel.

After a shower, cold though it was, I felt worlds better. I wandered down to the kitchen to see Tess had beat me to it. She was standing in front of the open cabinet doors, a confused look on her face. She glanced over her shoulder at me. "I don't know how to cook."

I laughed. "I'm not exactly great at it, either. But I'm sure together we can figure something out."

Tess and I pulled out some pasta we found in the back, and then there were some canned tomatoes. There was a garden out back, and we managed to pull together some greens, enough to make at least a small salad, along with some small cherry tomatoes. By the time everyone else was downstairs, we had a big bowl of pasta with sauce and salad ready to go. It might not have been the fanciest of meals, but honestly, Tess and I were feeling pretty proud of how it looked.

"All right, everybody, let's eat before it gets cold." Tess placed the plates and cutlery on the table.

I filled glasses with water and carried them over. Torr came over and helped. And then we all sat down and ate. No one really talked. We were too tired and too hungry. We hadn't had a good meal since we'd left Vera's. It had been small meals sometimes only a single fruit or some jerky when game was scarce.

Finally Donovan sat back, rubbing his stomach. "Man, that was good."

Tess licked her fingertips. "Not bad if I do say so myself."

I was feeling pretty happily sated too. "So, um, what's the plan here?"

Tess nodded. "I'll go speak with my cousin sometime soon, once we've rested a little bit. Just in case we need to leave quickly. He's not like the rest of the family, and I trust him. So I'll go see what he knows about what's happening back in Sterling Peak. Hopefully he'll be able to give us a heads-up, and then we can kind of decide what the next steps are going to be."

I nodded, even though it wasn't much of a plan. I liked the idea of just kind of relaxing for a few days.

"I'll go with you. Just in case," Donovan said.

Tess shook her head. "No. You can't. You're the second-in-command; you're too recognizable. That won't work."

"I can go," Torr said. "No one will even see me."

Tess turned to him, eyebrows raising. "You'll stay invisible the whole time?"

"Well, being I don't want to be killed, yes. But if you get into trouble, I'll be around."

"Good. That'll work." She turned back to the rest of us. "So it looks like we have a night off. There are some board games and books in the sitting room. There's even a chessboard."

Micah's eyes lit up. "Chess?"

Donovan cracked his knuckles. "I'm ready for a chess game."

Tess stood up and looked at Donovan. "And being Addie and I made dinner, I think it's only fair that those who didn't should wash the dishes."

"I knew there was a catch," Donovan grumbled.

He stood up and started collecting dishes and carrying them over to the sink. Noel, Micah, and I joined him, but Donovan ushered Noel and I away. "You two ladies out of here. This is man's work."

"You don't have to tell us twice." Noel linked her arm through mine and led me into the other room.

I wandered over to the bookshelf to read the titles there. There were a few that attracted my interest. Another few were on the Angel War, and I had already read them back at Vera's place. But the sight of them got me thinking. Graham and I were going to have to fight to the death. He'd nearly killed me once. I couldn't let him get that close again. If Graham died, I would be sad, and so would the others. But if I died, Noel and Micah would be lost. I couldn't let that happen to them. I couldn't let him kill me.

Which meant I was going to have to kill him.

"Addie."

I turned around as Tess walked into the room. "You okay?"

My gaze shot to the bookcase and the titles I was standing in front of. "Yeah."

Tess stopped next to me, dropping her voice after a quick glance at Noel, who was still scanning the stack of board games. "It's okay, you know."

"What is?"

"That you weren't able to kill him. I wouldn't have been able to do it, either."

"He's not going to stop. He's going to try and track me down. And anyone that's with me is in danger."

"I know. We've all accepted that risk." Tess paused. "It's okay if you've decided that you can kill him now too."

My head jolted up as I looked at her.

Tess gave me a sad smile. "I never thought I'd see the day when I would understand why someone would want to kill Graham Michael. He's always been the most upstanding, decent guy. But whatever that archangel did to him changed him. He's not the Graham I know. And the Graham I know wouldn't want to be used that way. He certainly wouldn't want to be a danger to you. The Graham I know would take it upon himself to kill this Graham to protect the ones he loves. So it's okay if you've made the same decision. I promise you if it comes down to it, I'll help you. I'll help you because it's what Graham would want."

Tears pressed against my eyes at the sadness in her tone as well as the determination. "Are you sure?"

Tess nodded, no doubt in her voice or face. "Yes."

CHAPTER 44

NOEL

IN HER MIND, Noel had always pictured Chicago like the pictures she'd seen in books. Tall skyscrapers, clean sidewalks, a bustle of activity. The reality was a huge disappointment. New Chicago was much smaller and much less impressive than the books.

There were no tall skyscrapers. At least, none that were currently inhabited. She could see the taller, decrepit ones in the distance. The sidewalks, where they still existed, had large cracks with weeds coming through. The buildings were much like Blue Forks: some of them crumbling, some of them makeshift. Noel, Tess, and Torr were heading toward a section that you could tell was set up more like Sterling Peak: full of money.

Noel hunched her shoulders and kept an eye on Tess, who walked on the opposite side of the street. They'd been at the cottage for three days now. It had given them a chance to recharge. Now, they were on their way to meet Tess's cousin.

Noel had insisted on going. She was good at not being seen when she didn't want to be, and she needed to see for herself if Tess's cousin could be trusted.

Plus, she had wanted to get into the city, see other people. But the trip hadn't been as freeing as she'd thought it would be. Instead, it had her feeling unsettled.

Invisible, Torr walked beside her. "Everything okay?"

"Yeah, it's just ... something feels off, you know?"

Noel had learned to pay attention to those feelings. She knew that words and a pretty smile could hide a dangerous intent. She believed that the air could often tell you more quickly than words when something bad was about to happen.

And right now, the air in Chicago felt dangerous.

She supposed it was possible that it was just that they hadn't been around a city like this in a long time. It'd been weeks, at least.

But she didn't think that was the entire reason. The people that they passed looked worried, scared. So far, everyone they passed had been Demon Cursed. It was easy to pick them out. Even though the Demon Cursed in Forks had a lot less than the Angel Blessed, there wasn't the same nervousness to their demeanor that she was seeing here. Was it just city life?

"I know what you mean. It feels wrong," Torr whispered.

A shout went up at the end of the street. Noel stopped and stared. An incredibly thin Demon Cursed man sprinted down the street, a look of terror on his face. Behind him, three members of the Seraph Force gave chase.

It was no contest. The man obviously wasn't in good shape. He was too thin, and there was a sick, gray pallor to his skin.

One of the Seraph Force tackled him to the ground.

Noel winced as the man's chin slammed into the ground, leaving a long cut. It bloomed with blood immediately. A second Seraph Force member helped wrestle the man to his feet.

The man trembled, shaking his head. "No, no, you can't do this. My family's sick. I'm the only one who can take care of them."

The third Seraph Force officer stared down at the man with

no compassion on his face. "You should've thought of that before you went into debt."

"But it's only one week's pay. I said that I would make it up next month. Mrs. Jophiel agreed."

"You know the rules. Anyone with any sort of debt can be indentured."

The man's mouth fell open. "But ... but my family ..."

The Ranger was unmoved by his plea, although the other two looked decidedly uneasy. "You can make your case to the Seraph Force leader. But it will take two weeks for a letter to get there and back."

"Two weeks? My family won't survive for two weeks."

"You should've thought of that before you borrowed the money. Now let's go."

The Ranger gripped the man by the arm and led him away. The man's shoulders drooped, his head bowed. He was the picture of absolute defeat. The other two Rangers exchanged another glance, then followed.

Noel's gaze darted across the street to Tess, who'd also stopped to watch the spectacle. Tess shook her head, warning Noel and Torr not to do anything.

Noel's blood boiled. That man was going to become an indentured servant just because he borrowed money? What the hell was going on?

"We need to get moving," Torr said.

Noel watched the man and the Seraph Force as they disappeared down the road. Something was very wrong here.

Very, very wrong.

CHAPTER 45

GRAHAM

GRAHAM LEANED over the side of the bed and pet Lady on the head. "Good morning, girl."

He looked over to the corner of the room where all of the puppies lay sleeping. Apparently, they hadn't been a figment of his imagination. Sometime in the last week, the puppies and their mama decided to take up residence in Graham's sickroom.

He didn't mind. In fact, he liked looking at the little pups. He swung his feet around the side of the bed and stood up, swaying for a moment, holding on to the wall.

Lady lifted up her head, tilting it to the side.

He gave her a smile. "I'm okay, girl."

Pushing off the wall, he shuffled to the door and headed down the hall. He didn't know the layout of the library very well. He'd spent most of his time in his bedroom, only taking trips to the bathroom and back again. Last night, he'd told himself he needed to get up and move around a little bit today. So he wandered down the hall and ended up in the kitchen.

Vera sat at a well-used wooden table writing in a notebook.

After closing the book and laying her pencil beside it, she looked up with a smile. "Well, look who decided to get out of bed. How you feeling?"

Graham sank into a chair at the other side of the table. "Like hell. But I figure I need to start to get moving."

Vera stood up. "Well, let me make you some eggs. Want some coffee?"

"I'll get it." Pushing himself back up, he winced as he made his way over to the coffee pot and carefully poured himself a cup. He took a sip and then carried it back to the table, ridiculously proud of himself for completing the simple task.

"You're healing nicely."

Graham nodded. Even though he felt horrible right now, he'd take that over those days when he wasn't in control any day of the week.

These last few weeks with only Vera, Lady, and her pups for company had actually been really nice. Vera had left him a stack of books to read, and Graham had devoured them all. Most had been on the Angel War. He wasn't sure if she was trying to tell him something or not, but the books had captivated his attention. He took another sip of coffee and then placed it on the table in front of him. "Vera, those books you left me on the Angel War, have you read them?"

Vera cracked an egg into the skillet with a nod. "Them and many, many more. There's a whole section in this library dedicated to the Angel War."

"Do you know about how I was gifted by Michael?"

Vera snorted. "Doesn't seem like much of a gift. But yes, I know what he did."

"Have you read about anything like that in any of the books? Is there a record of the angels having done that to other people?"

Vera flipped the two eggs in the skillet and then turned around, leaning against the counter, her arms crossed over her chest. "Not in the books downstairs, but I did hear about that during the Angel War. I'm sure there's a book somewhere that has an accounting of it."

"What do you know about it?"

Vera slipped the two eggs onto a plate and carried them over to the table, placing them in front of Graham with a fork.

"Thank you," he said.

Vera grabbed her own coffee mug and then took a seat across from him. "You're welcome. Now, let's see, there were rumors back during the war about the archangels using humans in that way. They would remove their free will and then send them out on missions."

Graham shuddered, remembering how it was to be lost in the darkness. He was unable to resist. He couldn't do anything except what the archangel ordered. And only occasionally could he see what was happening. And when he did, he wished he hadn't.

Vera eyed him. "I've never approved of that."

"Why did the archangels do it?"

Vera sighed. "Not real sure on that one. I think they were losing the fight against the demons, and they decided they needed to, I guess, increase the size of their army. From what I recall, the humans that they removed the free will of were all hardened soldiers. They were able to send them into battle with the demons and turn the war."

"I understand how important it is to fight the demons, but that way, through removing someone's humanity …" Graham shook his head.

"You have to remember angels weren't, and I'm guessing still aren't, fans of humans. We all talk about the Angel Blessed and Demon Cursed now, but there's no blessing that comes from the angels. They view humans as lesser than themselves. As far as they're concerned, angels are God's greatest creation, and humans are an inferior model. They have no compunction or care about whether or not humans are harmed."

"But that was how the Angel War really started, right? Lucifer and his jealousy of humanity?"

"Well, that is the tale. The angels led by Lucifer rebelled against God. They wanted to have what the humans had. They didn't want to be controlled at all times. And so they were banished from Heaven, and they fell."

"And then they turned into demons," Graham said.

Vera nodded. "For the archangels that remained in Heaven, that was proof of the wrongness of humanity. It was that jealousy of humanity's free will that led to the creation of the demons. Without free will, that never would've happened, and their brothers and sisters would have stayed in Heaven with them."

A niggling thought that had been rolling around Graham's mind for the last few days sprang to the forefront. "But how is any of that possible? If the angels didn't have free will, how did Lucifer rebel in the first place? Without free will, it should have been impossible, right?"

Vera smiled. "I see someone's been giving this some thought. And the simple answer is: yes. If God had chosen to, he could've removed the stirrings of free will completely from all the rebellious angels. But for some reason, he chose not to."

"But that means that on some level, and in some way, the angels are also capable of having free will."

"I believe that is true as well. But I think for many of them, they are soldiers first and foremost. They don't think for themselves. And they don't want to. They are so used to taking orders that the very idea of not taking orders for many of them is frightening."

Graham understood what she meant. He'd met more than a few Angel Blessed who were incredible soldiers on the battlefield, but when it came to their normal life, they struggled with all of the decisions they faced. "I get that."

"I believe you do. Now eat up those eggs before they get cold."

Graham smiled. "Yes, ma'am."

He bit into his eggs, grateful to have something solid. For the first few days he'd been awake, he'd had nothing but soup. Then he'd moved on to porridge. Eggs were one of the most solid thing he'd had so far. And they tasted absolutely delicious. He made quick work of his plate.

Vera's eyebrows rose. "It looks like your appetite's coming back. Another good sign."

Graham reached for his coffee mug and took a nice long drink. "Why do you think Michael came back now? And why make me go after Addie? She's never done anything but help humanity. If not for her, that demon horde would've overrun Blue Forks and Sterling Peak. She single-handedly held them back, allowing the people of Forks to escape."

"I never did get the full story from Addie and Torr about what happened there."

Graham settled back in his chair and told her everything. He told her about being the Seraph Force leader and how he'd learned that someone in Blue Forks was protecting people at night. He told her how he'd tried to track down that person and then finally discovered that it was Addie. He told her about moving them into his estate and watching over her, and finally, her defeating the demon horde and coming back to the estate just as Michael arrived and everything went sideways.

"You care about her a great deal," Vera said.

Graham's first instinct was to deny it. After all, the commander of the Seraph Force did not sit around talking about his feelings. But sitting here with Vera, he found himself just wanting to be honest. "More than I planned and more than I like to admit."

Vera nodded. "I think that's perhaps a good thing."

Graham stared at her in disbelief. "A good thing? How can that be a good thing? I'm supposed to kill her. I very well nearly did."

Vera shrugged. "It's good because you're human. The angels were able to rebel, and they weren't supposed to have any free will at all. I have to think that maybe, just maybe, you being human and caring for Addie gives you an edge."

Graham stared at her, an ember of hope enflaming in his chest. "You think I can resist?"

"I don't think that's up to me. I think that's up to you. Humans tend not to like to be told what to do. So I guess the question is: Are you a soldier who just follows orders, or are you someone who thinks for himself?"

"I don't think it's that easy."

"Oh, I don't think it's going to be easy at all. But that doesn't mean it's impossible."

Graham stared at her, the hope in his chest flaming brighter. But just as quickly, it was dashed. He hadn't even been able to be conscious for most of the time when his free will had been removed. How on earth was he supposed to be able to wrestle back control?

"You asked earlier why Michael returned at this time. I think it's because of Addie. Because of who her father is."

Graham frowned. "Her father? Who's her father?"

Vera's eyebrows rose. "You don't know?"

Graham shook his head. "I mean, I figure at least one of her parents was an angel, but I don't know which one. Marcus thought for a while it was Michael."

Vera snorted. "Oh, he wishes he was that lucky. No, Addie's existence is why you were activated. Michael is looking to take revenge."

Graham frowned. "Revenge? What's Addie done to him?"

Vera shrugged. "She exists. And her very existence is the antithesis of everything that Michael stands for."

The dots started to connect in Graham's mind. Dread bloomed in his chest. "She's the daughter of Lucifer."

"Yes, making her a symbol of everything Michael hates. As far as he's concerned, she is the reason for all of this destruction. You see, when the angels fell, it wasn't just to have the ability to make choices like humans. It was also to have the *lives* of humans, which meant being able to have children, to have a family. The angels are a family of a sorts, but it is not the same as having children or a significant other. And that's what the angels that fell wanted: that connection."

Graham frowned. "But why is that so bad? To want a family, to want a life?"

Vera reached over and patted his hand. "It's not. But for Michael, it was a slap in the face. It was as if they were telling him that everything he had done for his entire long life had been a waste. And he could not let that stand."

Graham frowned. "The way you tell it, it's like Michael's the bad guy in all of this rather than Lucifer."

Vera looked straight into his eyes. "Yes, it does sound like that, doesn't it?"

CHAPTER 46

NOEL

Noel felt more than a little shook after seeing the man get taken away by the Seraph Force. What was happening? Had Graham set all of this in motion? Things were never easy for the Demon Cursed, but now it seemed like things had gotten a whole lot worse.

"Heads up," Tess whispered from where she was crouched down next to Noel. They were on the roof of the building across from the print shop. It was a two-story brick building with a black awning over the front door and large windows.

The old print shop where Tess had set up the meeting had been owned by Tess and Peter's uncle. Tess explained that she and Peter had played there a lot when they were kids. The location would probably help convince him that the note she'd sent him requesting the meet was real.

Noel peered over the side and saw a blond man of average height, maybe a little on the short side, walk down the street toward the shop. He glanced around every now and then, checking his surroundings. Noel noted there was no one with him. That was good. Tess had requested that he come alone, but she hadn't been sure he would follow through.

Unseen by anyone but Noel, Torr walked about ten feet behind Peter.

Peter stopped at the door of the print shop. He hesitated under its awning before stepping inside. Torr quickly slipped down the alley next to the print shop and disappeared from view. A short time later, he reappeared on the other side, looked up toward the roof, and gave a nod.

"Torr says the coast is clear," Noel said.

"I still can't get used to the fact that he can go invisible. It's a whole new world, isn't it?"

A few minutes later, Tess and Noel were standing on the first floor of the old apartment complex that they had taken refuge on. Both of them had their hoods up and glanced around. Tess stared intently at the old print shop. "Is it still safe?"

Noel peered around her and glanced at Torr, who gave her another nod. "Yep. Still safe."

"Well, here goes nothing," Tess mumbled before she gripped the door handle and stepped outside. She moved quickly across the street and then slipped under the awning of the print shop and waited.

Noel took a breath, looking down the street both ways before she, too, darted across it. Noel put her hand on the handle of the door while Tess kept her hand on the hilt of her sword. After a nod from Tess, Noel flung the door open, and Tess burst inside.

Peter sat on a table across from the door, his feet swinging beneath him. He raised an eyebrow. "Very dramatic."

Tess glanced around the shop. "You alone?"

Peter slid off the edge of the table, wiping his hands on his pants. "Yes, as you requested. I wasn't sure it was you, but I was hoping."

He held open his arms. Tess's shoulders relaxed. She removed her hand from the hilt of her sword as she crossed the room. She wrapped her cousin in a hug. "It's good to see you, Peter."

He smiled, leaning his head into her. "You too, Apple."

Tess groaned, pulling away. "Don't start with that."

"Apple?" Noel asked.

Peter looked up, his blue eyes twinkling as he smiled at Noel. "When Tess here was young, she spent one entire summer eating nothing but apples. I'm not sure how she did it."

"I only did it because you told me I couldn't do it," Tess grumbled.

"And you proved me wrong."

Tess shook her head, but there was a smile on her face. "This is my friend Noel."

Peter swooped into a deep bow. "A pleasure, Miss Noel."

Noel couldn't help but smile. There was something inherently likable about Peter.

"How's Seth?" Tess asked. Tess flicked a glance at Noel. "He's Peter's much better half."

"That he is. And he's good, as always. But he's worried about you."

"You can't tell him you've seen me."

Peter's gaze became more serious. "What's going on, Tess? I got a missive weeks ago telling me to be on the lookout for you, Donovan, and some woman named Addison Baker. Graham said you were to be held and full force was authorized."

Peter's tone was bewildered as he stared down at his cousin before shooting a glance at Noel.

Tess sighed and leaned her hip against the table. "A lot's been going on. Graham is … Well, he's just not Graham anymore. Did you hear about the archangel's visit?"

Peter nodded slowly. "We heard the reports, but it just seemed so crazy. A large-scale demon attack followed by a visit from Michael? It's all true?"

Tess nodded wearily, and she pulled out a chair and took a

seat. "It's true."

It took her ten minutes to go through everything that had happened since the demon horde had attacked. Hearing it all laid out like that, Noel struggled to believe it had been real, and she'd been there.

"Are you okay?" It was the first question Peter asked, and it was telling. There was obviously a great deal of affection between the two cousins.

Tess reached out her hand and squeezed his. "I'm fine. I healed on the journey here. But we're trying to figure out where to go next. You won't tell anyone that you've seen us, will you?"

"You know better than to ask that. You're my family, Tess. The only family I actually like. Whatever you need, you've got."

"Well, right now, we need information. We need to know what's going on with the country," Tess said.

Peter blew out a breath. "Honestly, I'm still trying to wrap my head around that as well. We got a second missive shortly after the one from Graham. It was from D'Angelo, acting commander of the Seraph Force. It was a list of new laws that were to be enacted immediately."

"On the way here, we saw a man grabbed by the Seraph Force," Noel said. "They said something about him having a debt."

"Yeah, that's one of D'Angelo's new rules." Peter's tone indicated exactly what he thought of that particular rule. "If anyone is in debt to an Angel Blessed, they can be put into indentured servitude until the debt is paid off. But there's no rules, no accounting. An Angel Blessed can just make a claim, and then the person is essentially a slave until the Angel Blessed decides that they've paid enough."

"That's wrong," Noel said.

"Yes, it is. I don't know what the heck is going on. I don't know why Graham made D'Angelo acting, but I'm guessing this archangel business is underneath it all. Why isn't Donovan second?" Peter asked.

"He and Graham got into a fight," Tess said.

Peter's eyebrows rose. "Those two never fight, at least not seriously."

"It's been a long couple of months," Tess said wearily. For the first time, Noel could see the toll all of this had taken on her.

"There's more," Peter said.

Tess groaned. "I'd say I don't want to know, but…"

Noel listened in horror as Peter described all the restrictions now placed on the Demon Cursed. Food rations had been cut. Brutality had increased. There was a curfew, papers were required for Demon Cursed to move around Angel Blessed areas. The Seraph Force could search any Demon Cursed at any time and demand their papers. Not having them meant an automatic fine.

But that wasn't the worst of it. The fine could be paid by any Angel Blessed, which would in turn mean a debt was now owed to the Angel Blessed. And the Demon Cursed could be conscripted into servitude.

Peter ran a hand through his hair. "I'm trying to keep my force on the side of the right. But D'Angelo sent out a batch of replacements. He moved around some of my guys too. As a result, I've got people who've never worked with each other before. They don't know who to trust. And therefore, they're just following the rules as D'Angelo's laid them out. I wrote to Graham to see if I could get some information to find out why we're making these changes and lodging my complaint about the impact it was having on our society as a whole. Now I guess I know why I haven't heard back."

Tess exchanged a glance with Noel. "What about the search for Addison Baker?"

"I was getting missives about that every few days, and then they stopped. I guess that coincides with when Graham was injured." Peter paused. "Do you think he's still alive?"

"I don't know," Tess said wearily. "And I don't know whether to hope he is or pray he isn't."

CHAPTER 47

ADDIE

A TWINGE of pain echoed through my side as I took a seat on the couch. My injury still made it difficult to sit comfortably. The wagon had been unbearable at times. The wound had healed a great deal, but it wasn't completely back to normal yet.

I pictured Graham's face again, the look in his eyes when he looked up and saw me dropping toward him. It had been anger.

A shudder ran through me. I'd been plagued with images of him since that day. And yet deep down I still wanted to believe that somehow it would be all right. That somehow it would work out.

But the farther we got from Vera, the more I knew that was the true delusion. My injuries were proof that the prophecy was about to come true. And that only one of us would walk away from the next fight.

Needing a distraction from my thoughts, I walked into the kitchen and put on the kettle. There were some dried lemons in the cupboard. It wasn't as good as fresh, but I'd take what I could get. Once the water had boiled, I dropped a few lemon wedges in and then walked over to the front window. The house was dark, as night had started to fall. We hadn't seen anyone in our time here, but we still weren't taking any chances.

Donovan was upstairs sleeping. He'd barely slept for the whole trip here, or the last few weeks as the rest of us recharged. But he'd hit the wall today. I'd insisted he get some sleep. He was beyond exhausted. Micah had said he would wait with me for the others to get back, but he was curled up on the couch, oblivious to the world at this moment. But he had tried.

I took a sip of the tea, letting the warmth soothe me. The world outside was quiet. I wondered how long we'd be able to stay here. It was a nice home, quiet, simple. There was an old vegetable patch out back that looked like it would come alive come spring. If we were still here, we could have fresh produce every day.

I wasn't sure if that was good or bad. But I knew I needed to let myself daydream. I needed to hold on to the possibility that a normal future was an option still open to all of us.

I stood at the window, sipping lemon water and staring outside, letting my mind go blank. It took my mind a moment to catch up with what my eyes were seeing.

Horses entered the field in the distance. There were three of them. I moved to the side of the window and stared as the riders approached. It was possible the three were just cutting through the field on their way somewhere else.

But then the horses turned, heading straight for the cottage. I raced up the stairs and threw open the door to Donovan's room. Donovan bolted up right, his hair swinging into his face. He shoved it back. "What's going on?"

"Three horses headed this way."

Donovan rolled off the bed and grabbed his sword from the scabbard, belting it to his waist before pulling on his shirt.

I ran down the stairs. My heart pounded. Had the others been caught? Or was this just bad luck? Either way, we needed to be prepared. At the bottom of the stairs, I hurried into the living room. I crouched down next to Micah and shook his shoulder. "Micah. Micah."

He grumbled, his eyes slowly opening.

"Micah, someone is coming. I need you to hide."

His head jolted up. "What?"

"I need you to hide. Go to the barn, hide in the loft. I'll come get you when it's safe. Okay?"

He looked up at me with big eyes and then scampered off the couch and down the hall. Donovan moved to the side of the front window and looked outside. He frowned. "Noel's out there."

"What?" I hurried over to the window and peered outside.

He was right. Noel was one of the riders. Torr sat behind her. And Tess was there too. But the third rider I didn't recognize.

Donovan squinted, trying to make out the man's features in the dimming light. "I think that's Tess's cousin Peter."

"Why'd she bring him here?"

Donovan shrugged. "I don't know. But I know she trusts Peter. So let's go find out what's going on."

CHAPTER 48

I WASN'T sure what to make of Tess bringing Peter back. I trusted Tess. And I trusted her judgment. But I'd be lying if I didn't say I was anxious as they approached.

Noel rode next to her. She looked tense but not worried.

Torr sat behind Noel, his arms clasped around her waist. From the fact that Peter didn't look terrified and never glanced at him, I knew he hadn't revealed himself to Peter.

"Is Torr with them?" Donovan asked.

I nodded. "He's riding with Noel."

Donovan grunted. "Peter's a good man. And if Tess is bringing him here, there's something that she thinks we need to hear directly from him."

I understood what he was saying, but it still seemed like a risk.

Donovan and I stood in the courtyard. My hand itched to grab my sword from its scabbard, but I left it alone. If I needed to, I could take out Peter. I had no doubt about that. But I also knew I'd be taking out Tess's friendship as well. So I prayed that Tess was right about her cousin.

They trotted into the courtyard, and Tess met my gaze. She gave me a nod and a smile. "It's okay, guys."

She slid off her horse as Peter trotted his horse into the courtyard as well.

He was handsome, although not in the same league as Donovan and Graham. But there was something very friendly and open about his face, which made me wonder how exactly he was the major general of New Chicago.

Peter slid off his horse with practiced ease and grinned at Donovan. "I see you're still as ugly as ever."

"And I see you're still towering over all of your underlings," Donovan replied as he walked over and gave Peter a warm hug.

Peter barely reached Donovan's chin.

Donovan pulled back and nodded toward Addie. "Peter Uriel, this is Addison Baker."

Peter gave her a warm smile. "So you're the one they're making all the fuss about. No worries. I have no intention of revealing that you're here. Although I'm not sure that's going to be enough."

Noel and Torr slid off their horse. Noel walked over, holding the reins of her horse. "We— I mean, I'll take the horses."

I nodded and wasn't sure if Peter noticed that one of the horses seemed to be walking itself over to the stables.

Tess led everybody into the kitchen. I poured some glasses of iced tea as Peter and Donovan took seats at the kitchen table. I was too keyed up to sit.

Tess seemed to feel the same. She leaned against the counter next to me and finished her glass, then poured herself another, letting out a deep breath. "I needed that. Peter, tell them what's going on."

Once Peter began to speak, I understood why he was the head of New Chicago. In a quick, efficient recitation, he outlined the missives he'd received from Seraph Force headquarters.

My stomach dropped when I realized that Graham had sent notices and descriptions of me, Donovan, and Tess across the country. If they went anywhere near a city, they'd recognized by the local Seraph Force.

Peter continued after giving us a moment to soak in the information. "I'm afraid that's not the worst of the news. We've had an increase in demon attacks, a significant one, as in triple the usual. Just this morning, I had to increase the number of guards around the city. So if you're trying to slip out, it's going to be tougher."

"We noticed that," Donovan said. "It'll be tougher but not impossible."

"Well, there's one more thing. D'Angelo has insisted that all cities conduct home-to-home searches looking for you three."

I slumped back against the counter. Oh God.

Donavan leaned forward. "House to house? How long until they come here?"

"They've already been. You must have arrived just after. It was lucky you showed up when you did. But the searches are ongoing. And they are being conducted in every city. There's a country-wide manhunt out for you three. We've been told to continue the searches until Addie is found."

Now I really wished I had taken a seat at the table. I walked over, pulled out a seat, and sat down heavily. "Oh, great."

"And I'm afraid it gets worse."

Donovan shook his head. "Peter, you've said that about three times now."

"Yup, and each time, it got worse, didn't it?"

Donovan blew out a breath, nodding his head. "So how exactly does it get worse beyond what you've already told us?"

"D'Angelo's switched out my people, so that I don't know exactly who I can trust. And neither do my people. So we're having to follow his dictates while also constantly looking over our shoulders."

Donovan shrugged. "Well, that's doesn't seem too bad."

Peter shook his head. "I didn't get to the bad part yet. Another contingent arrived this morning. I didn't know if D'Angelo learned you guys were here or just guessed it, but I have another hundred Rangers. Normally, that would be great. But right now, that also means there will be a net over the city. No one will get in and out of the city without being seen. Even in the daytime."

"But you can pull some of those people back, right?" Tess asked. "The ones you know and trust. I mean, if we need you to?"

Peter shook his head. "I can, but it will throw up red flags. And I don't know that I can trust *all* of my people. I wouldn't turn my back on some of them. Besides, with the demons out there ..."

"It wouldn't be safe," I said. We couldn't trade our safety for others.

Donovan crossed his arms over his chest. "So you're saying getting out of the city without being seen is now going to be really difficult."

Peter's lips went thin. He shook his head. "No, I'm saying it's going to be impossible."

CHAPTER 49

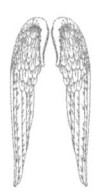

Donovan let out a muffled yell as he charged toward Noel. Noel slipped to one side as he thrust a wooden sword at her and then dodged his other attempt as he tried to tap her from the other side.

Frustration slanted across Donovan's face. He pulled his arm back to swipe across her ribs in what would have been a death blow if it had been a real sword.

I smiled, knowing which move Noel was going to use. It was one of her favorites and one that most didn't see coming.

Donovan's arm curled toward her. But instead of backing away, Noel twirled straight into Donovan's chest. Her arm wrapped around Donovan's as he completed the arc of his swing.

But Noel used his momentum to continue the swing. Donovan let out a yell as his feet came up from underneath him. He flew, and Noel used his lack of balance to twist the sword out of his hand.

Donovan landed with a thud. Noel placed the tip of the sword at his throat with a smile. "My point."

He looked up at her in a daze. "You need to show me that one."

Letting out a laugh, she stepped back so that Donovan could get up.

I couldn't help but grin as Noel glanced over at me. "Nice."

"I had a good teacher." Noel handed Donovan the sword hilt first but kept her twinkling eyes on me.

"Way to go, Noel!" Micah clapped as he sat next to Torr, who'd once again cloaked himself. Torr gave her a thumbs-up. Noel's cheeks flushed red at all the attention.

Donovan glanced up at the sky. "Looks like we'll lose the light soon."

Wiping the dirt from his pants, Torr stood up. "We should head in. It will be harder to see anybody coming in the dark."

The light-hearted mood that had been over our group just moments ago disappeared even faster than the dwindling sunlight. It had been two weeks since we'd arrived at the cottage. Each day, we'd waited, expecting some of Peter's troops to appear in the distance. We had a plan for how we were going to escape, depending on what direction Peter's people came from.

But that ended up not happening. Peter had contacted us a few days ago to say that the demon attacks had ratcheted up to such a level that it was interfering with D'Angelo's search orders.

Not that we had been resting on our laurels. Each day, we trained, without fail. Donovan, Tess, and I did reconnaissance missions every other day, trying to see if there would be an easier way to slip through the net that had been thrown around Chicago. But it looked worse and worse. During the day, the Seraph Force Rangers were spread out all over the place, in some areas only twenty feet away from one another. And at night, the demon attacks seemed to be happening everywhere.

As each day passed and the news got more dire, I couldn't help but think about what I had read in Vera's library about the start of the Angel War. At the beginning, the demon attacks had increased the same way. Were we about to enter into another Angel War? Would the demons overrun us? Would the archangels come to our rescue this time? And how many humans would be lost in the process?

So far, we had been lucky. No one, not human or otherwise, had found us at Tess's old family home.

But I knew that was exactly what it was: luck. We couldn't count on that lasting forever. At the same time, even if we managed to get out of New Chicago, I still had no idea where we could possibly go. All the major cities had been locked down the way New Chicago was. They were all experiencing an increase in demon attacks as well. We could go to one of the smaller cities or villages we saw, but we'd definitely cause a stir showing up in place like that. There was no way we would be able to slip in unnoticed, which meant that word would get back to Graham.

My heart tightened at the thought of him. Once again, I pictured him lying on the ground. I knew that the time was coming when the two of us would have to meet. We couldn't keep running. It would be too dangerous for all of us. But I wasn't looking forward to what was to come.

Tess appeared in the doorway, wiping her hands on a towel. "Dinner."

Donovan hid his grimace. Noel did as well, although she hid it better than the others. Tess had decided that being we were spending a lot of down time here at the family cottage, she was going to try to figure out this cooking thing.

The experiments had not all been successes. In fact, some of them had been downright awful, but I had to admit that she definitely had jumped into being the family cook with gusto, if not skill. Even though I managed to keep my face impassive, my stomach rolled at the thought of what new concoction she'd created for dinner. Last night, she'd mixed cinnamon and coconut with eggs over a trout. I could swear the aftertaste was still in my mouth.

"Uh, what did you make?" Micah asked innocently.

"Oh, just some pasta and sauce tonight. I didn't have any ideas for something new."

Micah grinned as he hurried into the house. "That sounds great."

And I wasn't lying. My stomach rumbled at the thought of it. Noel trailed in after Micah, looking a little more eager for dinner.

Donovan gave me a look.

"I'll be right there," I said. With a nod, he headed in after the other two.

Once I was sure everyone was inside, I turned to Torr. "Anything?"

Torr had been slipping in and out during the day, doing reconnaissance. He did the same at night—despite my protestations that it was too dangerous. During the day, he could keep himself hidden and out of reach of humans, even as he slipped in and out of buildings to listen to their conversations. But I worried at night that a demon would come across him.

"They're still doing the searches house by house like Peter said. And the demon attacks have ratcheted up. It seems like there's about eight a night in New Chicago alone."

I winced at the high number. "Casualties?"

"There's usually at least one missing from each attack."

"And Peter?"

"I think he's trustworthy. At least, I haven't heard anything or seen anything that would suggest otherwise. Earlier I followed him. He stopped a Seraph Force member from arresting a young mother for debt. And then he paid her debt. It was ... kind."

I knew those words didn't come easily from Torr. And if Peter had earned his tentative seal of approval, then that was saying something. "What about the search for us?"

"Peter has them searching, but it seems like he's directing those efforts away from us. He's buying us time. Plus, with the demon attacks, the Force is stretched pretty thin. But the Rangers have managed to intercept at least half of the attacks in the last week.

In most of those cases, they've managed to take down the demons before too much damage has been done. But it's still not a good situation."

"No, it definitely isn't."

New Chicago was a bigger city than Sterling Peak, which would explain the higher number of demon attacks. But Peter himself said this number was unusual. That in the last two months, the numbers had tripled.

And I couldn't help but recognize that the numbers had increased right after the demon horde attacked Blue Forks and Sterling Peak. Something was definitely going on.

And I felt guilty because all I could manage to do was stay here in hiding. People were dying, and I couldn't chance going out to help because if I was seen, word would get back to D'Angelo, and probably Graham.

I was reaching the point where I could no longer sit back. Graham and I were going to have to come face-to-face. And it would have to happen soon. I'd been putting it off not because I was worried about Graham killing me. If push came to shove, I was the stronger fighter. No, I'd been putting it off because I didn't want to kill him. And what if, when the time came, I couldn't do it, like before?

The demon situation made it clear, though, that I didn't have the right to think that anymore. How many people had died during the time I'd been hidden away? How many of them could I or Donovan or Tess have saved? Or if Graham had killed me and then returned to himself, how many could *he* have saved? Did I really have the right to place my life or his above anybody else's?

At the same time, I was so angry. People were dying because the archangel Michael decided that I was an enemy. And I still had no idea why. I had no memory of my time before Blue Forks. And I could not imagine that I was actually on the side of the demons, even if they had been created by my father.

My father. I had no feelings for him one way or the other. He wasn't even a smudge of a memory. So how could I be responsible for whatever he had done eons ago? Besides, all I knew about him was that he was the leader in Hell and that certainly wasn't going to win me over.

"Addie?" Torr asked.

I looked over at him, pulled from my thoughts. "Hey. Sorry, just kind of got lost there for a minute."

"You want to finish this, don't you?"

I looked at him and then back over at the sun as it sank below the horizon. Around it, the sky was lined with streaks of orange, pink, and red. "Want to? No. But before too long, I'm going to have to."

CHAPTER 50

GRAHAM

Graham slid open the door to the supermarket. Lucky, one of the pups, trotted at his side. He closed the door behind the two of them. Lucky trotted forward, making his rounds. Lucky and Graham had gotten into a morning routine where they would go to the barn and feed the animals together.

Well, Graham fed the animals. Lucky would go from stall to stall "saying" good morning to everyone. It was kind of amazing. Graham had never seen a dog that liked other animals so much.

Ahead, Lucky trotted over to one of the horse stalls. He lifted himself up on his back legs, leaning his two front paws on the stall door, straining his neck up as high as he could go.

The white horse that Graham had named Beauty leaned her head down over the bottom half of the door and nuzzled Lucky's nose. Lucky's little tail beat furiously at the friendly greeting.

Then he jumped down and hurried over to the next stall to repeat the process.

All the animals seemed to like Lucky's visit. They all stood at the edge of their stalls waiting for their turn to say good morning to him.

Graham turned to the right and grabbed the wheelbarrow and pitchfork from the tool closet. He rolled it to the back of the stable where the fresh hay was piled up.

After loading the wheelbarrow, he doled out the hay and then refilled everybody's water. He spread out some feed for the chickens and gave the pigs the leftovers from last night's dinner, plus some oats. Then he began tidying up a little bit.

Once finished, he opened the paddock gates and led the cows out back so they could wander the pasture and feed themselves. Then he let the rest of the animals out into the pasture so they could all stretch their legs. They'd stay outside most of the day. In all, the morning chores took about ninety minutes.

Graham loved it. There was something so simple, so honest about this morning routine. Lucky let out a happy bark and sprinted for the pasture. He tripped over the lip of the doorway and tumbled head over heels. Unbothered by the clumsiness, he got right back up and made a beeline for the cows, happily running laps under and around them.

Graham leaned back against the post underneath the shade of a tree, watching. Lucky would be done in another five minutes, and then he would curl up next to whichever animal had stopped moving.

Right now he was trying to grab the tail of Bessie, the cow matriarch, who was ignoring him while contentedly munching on some grass. The rest of the cows didn't even blink at the puppy's antics. They'd all grown used to them by now.

Vera walked up and leaned on the other side of the fence. "He seems to be having a great time."

"He always does," Graham said. He felt Vera's gaze on him.

"You all right this morning?" she asked.

Graham was about to nod his head and say yes like he always did, but instead he shook it. "It won't be long now," he said softly.

He'd already told Vera about feeling the darkness encroaching on his mind. He was barely able to hold it back. Last night, he hadn't slept because he was afraid that his control would slip while he was asleep, and the darkness would seep in. So instead, he'd sat down and written some letters.

"I left some letters in my room. Could you make sure they get to Donovan and Addie?"

"I'll make sure," Vera said.

"Thank you. For everything. These last couple of weeks have really meant the world to me. I don't think I can ever thank you properly."

"No thanks necessary. I've enjoyed having you around. And the pups have really enjoyed having you around as well."

In the pasture, Lucky rolled onto his back in front of the bull. The bull snorted at him and then leaned down to sniff Lucky's face. Lucky's tail wagged harder at the attention.

Graham couldn't help but smile. "They've been good company."

"Sometimes animals make the best company. They don't talk back. They don't argue. They live in the moment, not the past, not the future. They stay right in the here and now. Humans could learn a lot from that."

Graham nodded, realizing that being here had allowed him to do that too. He still thought about what he'd done to Addie and what would happen in the future. But for the most part, by pure force of will, he'd been able to shove those thoughts aside and just live in the here and now. It had given him some peace, at least, until a few days ago, when the darkness had begun to seep back in.

Vera stared at him, her gaze intense. "Remember what I said about when the darkness takes hold, right?"

"Not to forget who I am," he said. But he knew that wasn't possible. He was, at best, a witness to his actions.

A pounding in his head began. He winced, rubbing his forehead.

"Graham?"

"Just a headache."

The pounding increased. He felt like his brain was trying to split in two. His vision blurred. He dropped to his knees, and his hands shot to either side of his head as he rocked.

"Graham!" Vera reached through the fence to touch his shoulder.

He shook his head. "No. Don't. Stay back."

The darkness swept into his brain, overriding everything, even the pain. His eyes snapped open, his back straightened, and he stood up.

"Graham?"

Graham turned to stare at Vera. She had bandaged his wounds. But she knew nothing of where Addie had gone, meaning she was of no use to him. He turned and strode toward the barn. He needed a horse.

A small puppy hurried up to him. Scampering after him, it leaned against his leg as he started to pull open one of the stall doors. Graham kicked it away.

The dog let out a little cry and then scampered low on all four paws, taking refuge behind the wheelbarrow.

Graham discounted the small animal from his thoughts, even as a small twinge of something pounded in the corner of his mind.

But none of that mattered. He'd lost too much time trying to hunt down Addie. He needed to regroup. He needed to come up with a plan.

After placing a blanket on the horse's back, Graham grabbed the saddle from the side of the stall and slung it onto the horse. In less than three minutes, he was riding down the main street of the old town. He passed the old woman again. She didn't say anything, just watched him go by.

He was only a half mile beyond Pitkin's last standing building when he saw a bright light in the sky. His horse startled, but Graham kept control of it as the light landed a few hundred yards ahead of him. Graham dug his heels into the side of the horse, setting it to a canter. He slowed the horse to a walk when he spotted Michael.

The archangel looked like a perfect specimen of humanity. Smooth dark skin, high cheekbones, and dark eyes. He stood waiting, his arms crossed over his chest, accentuating his biceps.

Graham dismounted, holding on to the reins as he approached the archangel.

"I have been unable to sense you," Michael said.

"I was injured. I only just now completed my healing."

Michael narrowed his eyes. "*Where* have you been healing?"

Graham waved his hand toward Pitkin. "A small town. An old woman took care of me."

"And who is she?"

"No one of consequence. But I found Addie. I was close to killing her, but she got the drop on me."

"How?"

Graham hesitated. "I underestimated her. I did not think she would go for the kill. I will not make that mistake again."

"Good. Because I know where she is."

CHAPTER 51

ADDIE

THE HOUSE WAS STILL dark as I approached. I made my way quietly around the side, gazing at each of the windows. There was no movement, no light.

I'd left the window in the kitchen unlatched. I made my way to it, glancing over my shoulder. All was silent. Carefully, I inched the window up. Gripping the frame, I hiked one leg through then hauled myself in, ducking under the window as I pulled my other leg in.

I stepped to the ground, but my left foot got caught on the frame. I stumbled, bouncing on my right leg to catch my balance and nearly landing on my face. After managing to wrestle my leg free, I slumped back against the wall.

"Graceful."

I yelped, my wings unfurling and flaming for a split second. That split second was long enough to see Donovan and Tess sitting at the dining room table.

My hand flew to my throat as if to keep my heart, which

pounded heavily, from escaping. "What are you two doing? Trying to give me a heart attack?"

Tess scoffed. "Oh, sure, *we're* trying to give you a heart attack. You're the one who snuck out of the house in the middle of the night and then snuck back in."

I winced. "Yeah, sorry about that. It's just ... what Torr said earlier about the demon attacks and the people really needing help got to me. I had to see if I could do something."

"And did you?" Donovan asked.

"Yes. A family about four miles down the road. Three demons went after the mother. She was coming home from work."

"Work? This late?"

Anger boiled through me as I pictured the poor woman's face. "Yeah. She's a Demon Cursed. And apparently her Angel Blessed employer said she would claim she was in debt to her if she didn't stay late."

Donovan cursed softly.

"Did she see you?" Tess asked.

"It was dark. She never saw my face." I tugged on the scarf around my neck. "This hid the lower half of my face anyway. And I didn't use my wings. So she knows someone helped her, but she won't never be able to identify me. And I asked her not to say anything."

"That was incredibly reckless," Tess said.

I pulled out a chair and slipped into it. "I know. It's just..."

I ran a hand through my hair, trying to put into words how helpless and frustrated I'd been feeling ever since Peter first explained about the increasing demon attacks, and then Torr had reinforced the direness of the situation. "I know it's not reasonable, but I feel like this is all my fault. I feel like somehow the increasing demon attacks has something to do with me and that stupid prophecy."

"That makes no sense," Donovan said.

I blew out a breath. "I know. I know. But at the same time, I'm keeping you two from defending people from the demons as well. That's three of us out of the game, four if we include Graham. And right now it seems like the world needs every soldier it can get."

My eyes had adjusted to the dark by this point, and I realized that both Donovan and Tess were completely suited up for battle. Each had their sturdier jackets on, plus their bows, a quiver of arrows, and their swords. "Was there a problem here? Why are you guys all weaponed up?"

Donovan squirmed in his seat. "Well, you know, we just kind of thought ..."

I narrowed my eyes. "You two were going out to help."

"You're not the only one who feels guilty and useless," Tess grumbled.

I closed my eyes, even more guilt piling on me now. Tess and Donovan had been part of the Seraph Force for years. By helping Noel, Micah, and me, they'd been pulled out of that life. If it was hard for me to sit back and not help, I could only imagine how much worse it was for them.

"I'm sorry. This is all my fault. If I had only ..." I let my words dwindle off. I wasn't sure how to finish that statement. If I had only what? Not woken up on the beach? Not protected the people of Blue Forks? Not run away from Graham?

"If you only had let Graham kill you?" Tess asked softly. "We don't blame you for any of this. As far as I'm concerned, the only one to blame is the archangel Michael."

"Tess," Donovan said in a shocked tone.

She crossed her arms over her chest. "What? He flies down, takes over *your* best friend, and sends the rest of us on the run so that Graham doesn't kill Addie. How is he *not* the villain in the story? Yeah, I get the whole 'Addie is the daughter of Lucifer' thing, but that's not all she is. For angel's sake, we just caught her sneaking in after helping some other people. Because of Michael, she has to *sneak out* to save people. So if you want to explain to me how the archangels, and Michael especially, make this world a better place, I'd love to hear it. Because right now, I really can't see it. And I'd choose Addie over any of them any day of the week."

I stared at Tess in both disbelief and gratitude. I'd never heard anyone speak ill of the archangels. They were always the heroes in the stories. Which was part of the reason why I felt so guilty. After all, if an archangel had targeted me, there must be something really wrong with me, right?

But Tess put into words the thoughts that had been swirling around in the back of my mind. Why did the archangel want me dead? I mean, maybe I was the world's worst human being before I woke up on that beach, but I didn't think so. I couldn't remember my life before then, but unless I experienced a radical personality transformation, I just didn't see how I was worthy of being enemy number one on Michael's most wanted list.

Donovan let out a slow breath. "You're not wrong. I don't see why Addie's the target of all this, either. But it doesn't change the fact that her going out to help other people is a risk. We're on the run to keep her from getting killed. Her going out there does not help with that."

Tess crossed her arms over her chest. "Yeah, but like us, sitting on the sidelines while other people need help is not in her DNA, even if her DNA came from the Devil himself."

I looked at Tess in the dim light, so incredibly grateful I could call her friend. I hadn't had any friends in Blue Forks, just acquaintances. And it was amazing how much her support and understanding right now meant.

"Now," Tess said, "I think we all agree that sitting on the sidelines is no longer an option. People need help. And we can provide it. We just need to come up with a plan for how we can do that without being seen."

"What do you have in mind?" Donovan asked.

"I think we should switch out who goes out every other night," Tess said. "You and I will go together. Addie will go on her own.

That way either she's here to protect the kids or both of us are here to protect the kids."

My heart lifted at the idea, and relief poured through me at the thought of actually being out doing something helpful. "That sounds great."

"But we can't go out for more than a few hours, no matter what," Donovan said. "The chances of us getting caught or seen rise with each additional hour we're out there. We go out when it's dark, and we come back well before dawn."

Both Tess and I nodded our agreement. I smiled. "Okay. It looks like we're back in the saving people business."

Tess grinned. "About damn time."

CHAPTER 52

The next two weeks were incredibly tiring but also incredibly fulfilling. As agreed, Donovan, Tess, and I switched out on nightly patrols. The nights when Donovan and Tess were out, Torr stayed up with me to keep an eye on the house and to make sure that there were no problems while we waited for Donovan and Tess to return.

Each night, we dispatched at least two demons, and all of us felt better for being able to contribute.

But the reports from Peter made it clear that our help was a mere drop in the bucket compared to what was needed. Demon attacks were increasing exponentially. We still hadn't figured out why. There hadn't been answers in those books back at Vera's library about what had caused the origins of the Angel War. And that was critical information right now.

Because it seemed like we were right on the cusp of a second one.

Except the angels hadn't appeared. The only angel that had been seen so far was Michael. There'd been no reports of any other archangel sightings across the globe.

I was caught between hoping the archangels never appeared—which made me feel selfish—and praying for humanity's sake that they appeared, which only increased my fear. Because if the other archangels arrived, I had to assume that they'd be on the side of their brother Michael.

Which would not be very good for me.

Now I stood at the dining room window, staring out into the night. Torr was on the other side of the house in the living room, keeping watch as well.

I blinked, rubbing my eyes. Donovan and Tess should be back soon. It was getting close to the four-hour mark. We were all very careful about sticking to our preset plan.

I stifled a yawn. The late nights were catching up with me. As soon as those two got back, I was going to pass out. Last night, I'd had trouble going to sleep, the image of the victims I'd been too late to save the night before running on an unending reel through my mind. I'd saved at least a dozen people, but it didn't even the scales as far as I was concerned. There were still families grieving right now.

A shadow shifted in the corner of the yard. I frowned, trying to see what had caused the movement. There was an old tree just outside the tall fence. Sometimes that shifted with the wind, making it appear as if people were in the yard. I'd mistaken the shadows more than once for a human.

Torr appeared in the dining room doorway. "They're coming."

There was no urgency or fear in his voice, which meant he was talking about Donovan and Tess. I nodded, not taking my gaze away from the shadows in the corner of the yard.

"Addie?"

"I saw something. I'm sure it's nothing but ..."

From the corner of my eye I saw Tess and Donovan's horses appear as they made their way toward the house. My gaze flicked to them for only a second.

But that second was at the same moment the demons emerged from the shadows. There were four of them. In the dim light, I couldn't make out their color, but they were immense. Two of them had large horns, which meant were older and more experienced.

I grabbed the window and flung it open as my wings burst free. I dove through the window before Torr could even say a word. "Demons!"

Donovan and Tess pulled sharply on their reins. Their heads swiveled from side to side, looking for the threat. The two smaller demons at the back paused, hearing my call.

I soared toward them, intent on my prey.

A large hand burst from the dark next to the house. It wrapped around my left wing, yanking me back. I cried out, feeling as if my wing was about to be ripped from my body. The demon shifted its grip to the back of my head and pulled me up. I'd never seen one this large. It had to be close to eight feet. In the dim light, its skin looked gray rather than green. With its wide face, it leered down at me. "There you are. Abbadon's been looking for you. He'll be so happy when I bring you back as a pet."

I slipped my sword from my sheath. "Sorry, I'm not interested in being anyone's pet."

I opened my wings wider, creating a space between them.

The demon frowned. "What—"

I plunged my sword back and through the demon's chest.

It's mouth let out a small "oh." It loosened its grip on the back of my head. I wrenched myself free, keeping my grip on the sword, which glowed now with fire. I dropped my weight to the ground as the sword, firmly gripped in my hand, ripped down the creature's chest.

As my feet touched down, I jerked the sword free.

The demon stumbled back, staring at me before it crashed to the ground, bursting into ash. I didn't give it another thought as I whirled and flew toward the other four. Torr had already sprinted from the house to join the fight. Donovan and Tess were taking on the two large demons while Torr fought off the two smaller ones. My heart leapt into my throat as Noel launched herself from the front of the house and sliced through the back of the thighs of one of the smaller demons attacking Torr.

It cried out in pain, whirling around. Noel ducked, rolling to avoid its wild swing. She rolled back to her feet, her sword still in front of her. Noel parried the creature's thrusts, managing to keep herself out of its reach. And each time it reached for her, it pulled an arm back with more cuts on it.

I put on a burst of speed and plunged my sword through its back, punching it out through the front. Its back arched, and its arms fell wide as I yanked my sword out.

"Torr, drop!" I ordered as I turned in the air. With an arching swing, I decapitated the smaller demon. Its body stood upright for a moment, as if confused as to where its head had gone. Then it, too, crashed to the ground in a lifeless heap.

Tess and Donovan had taken out one of the larger demons. They now circled the remaining one. It laughed as it looked up, meeting my gaze as it started to fade. "Abbadon will reward me well for finding you."

I rushed forward. "Don't let it go!"

But Donovan was already moving. He plunged his sword into the creature's stomach as Tess plunged hers through its back. The creature solidified again. Both yanked their swords out. The creature dropped to the ground, disappearing into a ball of ash.

"Everybody okay?" Donovan asked.

I scanned Noel, but she didn't have any noticeable injuries. But Torr's forearms were scratched up something fierce. "We need to get those cleaned up."

He nodded numbly.

"I'll take him inside," Noel said.

I gave her a nod and a small smile. "Thanks. And you did great."

Noel gave me a small smile back before helping Torr back into the house. I turned to Donovan and Tess.

"Where the heck did those four come from?" Tess asked, wiping her brow.

"Five. There was one other one closer to the house." I rolled my shoulder, my wings still smarting from its grip. "They appeared right as we caught sight of you guys."

"Good thing you were keeping watch."

"Yeah. But why were they here? I mean, this house is completely isolated."

"They must be switching up their game," Tess said. "Going after more isolated homes."

Which meant they had to have bigger numbers than we realized. Sending demons out into the countryside would be a waste of time with better pickings in cities and neighborhoods.

"How'd it go tonight?" I asked.

They both looked a little worse for wear. Tess's shirt was ripped at the shoulders, and there was the blood was splattered across both of them.

"It was a rough one. We dispatched six before we came home," Tess said

"*Six?* That's crazy."

"It's like the valve's been released. They're pouring out," Donovan said.

I stared out into the night. "We can't keep doing this."

"Fighting them?" Donovan asked.

I shook my head. "No, staying *out* of the fight. I know what will happen if I'm seen. I know it'll draw Graham here. But I feel like I'm trading my life for other people. I can't do that anymore."

"It's not just Graham," Donovan said. "The entire Seraph Force is looking for you as well."

"I know. But there's got to be a way we can be a bigger help than just a couple of hours a night. People are dying."

Tess sighed, her gaze straying to where the largest demon had turned to ash. "I'll get word to Peter. I'll see if he can identify some people he trusts. Maybe we can work over in their section and they can keep it quiet."

I nodded, feeling better at even the idea of doing more. "Okay. Let's talk to Peter."

CHAPTER 53

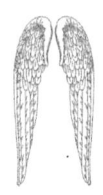

I FELT UNSETTLED. It wasn't just because of the demon attack at the house last night. It was as if something in the air had changed.

We were all waiting. Tess was going to slip into town later and contact Peter to tell him we needed to talk.

But until then, there was nothing to do. We were all just trying not to bump into each other. For the first time, the house felt small. The walls felt like they were closing in.

I wandered around the kitchen, opening cabinet doors and then shutting them again. There wasn't a lot of food, but I was used to that. And I wasn't really hungry anyway.

"What are you looking for?" Noel asked.

I turned and saw her standing in the kitchen doorway. I shrugged. "Nothing. Something. I don't know."

Noel took a seat at the table. "What do you think is going on?"

"With the demons? I don't know that either."

Noel shook her head. "No, with Graham. He should be healed by now, shouldn't he?"

I nodded stiffly. "Yeah, probably."

"Do you think he'll find you?"

I bit my lip, weighing my answer. I wasn't sure what to say. I mean, we had managed to slip past him in Blue Forks, and we'd stayed hidden from him for a while at Pitkin. But eventually he would catch up with us, just like he did before.

And I still didn't quite understand how that worked. The archangel should be able to tell where we were, right? Couldn't he sense it somehow?

"I don't know. We'll probably have to move soon. But I'm just not sure where we can go. Nothing seems like a safe option right now."

"But we're all going together, right?"

I sighed, my fingers splayed on the table before me. I wanted to say no. I wanted to leave Noel, Torr, and Micah somewhere safe. But the problem was, I didn't know what was safe anymore. With Graham looking for me and an increase in demon attacks, it seemed everywhere I could leave them would be a problem. I wanted to wrap them up and tuck them away from all of this but that simply wasn't an option.

So I nodded. "Yes. We go together."

Noel reached over and squeezed my hand. "We've got this, you know."

I didn't share her optimism, so I merely squeezed her hand back and gave her a smile.

I looked up as Donovan appeared in the doorway. "Peter's riding up."

I stood up, concern rushing through me. "Did Tess already contact him?"

Donovan shook his head. "No."

Oh no. I turned to Noel. "Get the go bags and get the horses ready. Just in case."

She looked like she wanted to argue, but after a moment's hesitation, she nodded and disappeared down the hall. I heard her making her way up the stairs, calling for Micah and Torr.

Donovan was already at the front door when I reached it. He opened it, holding it wide for me to pass through. Tess stood in the yard, her arms crossed, her legs braced as Peter raced across the field.

I swallowed as he approached us and then straightened my back. Something was definitely going on. He barely slowed as he approached us. He pulled the horse to a jarring stop and leapt off.

Tess stepped forward. "What happened?"

Peter took a deep breath to control his ragged breathing. "Graham's here."

CHAPTER 54

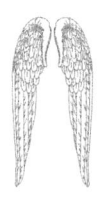

TWO HOURS EARLIER

GRAHAM

New Chicago had once been a bustling city full of people, life, and energy. Now it was just a wasteland. Many of the taller buildings had collapsed in on themselves. Only the Demon Cursed dare to live amongst them, and those were the true outcasts of society. New Chicago had been built over the ashes of the old. The Seraph Force had cleared out an area along the lake and started to rebuild after the Angel War. Now it had a thriving population of 10,000 people.

Graham had been to New Chicago a half dozen times in his life. He had family there. This branch of the Michaels was much older, though. They had no members currently in the Seraph Force, although his great uncle was still on the Council of Light for New Chicago. But Graham had no intention of stopping to see family. He was on a mission.

The archangel had left him shortly after he found him in

Pitkin and told him he needed to head to New Chicago. The trip here had been long and brutal. He'd hit a hailstorm with hail the size of softballs that had left him bruised before he found a cave to take refuge in. There'd also been downpours that made the ground too dangerous to cross, forcing him to take longer roads.

And with each passing day, he felt that presence in his mind growing larger. But every once in a while, he could feel the slip.

Graham watched all of it while tucked away in the corner of his own mind. He felt like he was beating his head against a brick wall, trying to escape the archangel's order. It didn't matter how much he screamed or wailed inside his mind—his body continued on its mission.

But Vera's words had given him hope. The angels had rebelled. They had been able to make decisions for themselves. Graham had to be able to do the same thing.

He'd tried this whole long journey, but so far, he'd had no luck. But he would continue to try. He couldn't watch as the archangel forced him to kill those he cared about. He was still haunted with images of Addie bleeding from the arrow he'd shot in her side.

He crossed into New Chicago and approached the gate. Two Rangers blocked his way. "Papers," one of the men demanded. The darkness slammed over him.

Graham glared down at him. "Careful how you speak."

The other Ranger grabbed her colleague's arm and tugged on it, pulling him back. "Commander Graham. No one said you would be arriving, sir."

"Tell Major General Peter that I'm on my way."

"Yes, sir. Right away." She took off at a run.

The other flicked a glance at Graham. "I'm sorry, sir. I didn't recognize you."

Graham didn't even bother responding as he walked his horse past him, then dismounted. His horse had been dragging for the last couple of miles. "I need a fresh horse."

"Yes, sir, of course. Take mine." The Ranger pointed to a chestnut-colored horse attached to a pole only ten feet away.

Graham flicked his reins at the man and strode over to the other horse, mounting it quickly. He set a quick pace, heading for the Seraph Force headquarters. Major General Peter Uriel was cousins with Tess. And they were close. That could be a problem.

But Graham was counting on that closeness.

Graham wended his way through the New Chicago streets, not really paying attention to his surroundings except to look for danger. He didn't register any of the faces as he passed. Angel Blessed or Demon Cursed, they were irrelevant to his world right now. All that mattered was finding Addison.

The archangel was convinced that Addison was in New Chicago. He couldn't say where exactly, but he was sure of it.

Graham did wonder: If the archangel was so sure of where Addison was now, why hadn't he been able to tell him earlier? It would have saved a lot of time in trying to track her down.

But he supposed the ways of the archangels were not his to understand.

Ahead, he saw the Seraph Force headquarters, a three-story brick building that fanned out, with ten windows along the front. It was surrounded by a metal fence. Beyond the house was a huge training area and separate barracks for the Rangers.

Graham cantered up to the guardhouse and slipped from the horse. A Ranger stood at attention.

"Commander Graham. It's good to see you, sir."

Graham ignored him as he strode toward the front door. A Ranger was just stepping out of the main door as he approached. She held the door open. "Commander Graham, sir."

Once through the door, Graham made his way to the left. The major general's office would be at the far end of the hall. All of the Seraph Force academies were designed the same way. His boot steps echoed off the heavy tile floor. The door to Peter's office was open. He sat at his desk and came to his feet when Graham strode in.

Graham pulled off his gloves and nodded to Peter. "Major General."

Confusion crossed Peter's face for a split second before he covered it. "Graham. It's good to see you again."

"Have you had any sightings of Addison Baker?"

If Peter was surprised by the lack of small talk, he didn't show it. "No. None of my people have reported seeing her or any of the others listed on the arrest warrant."

Graham doubted that was true. He narrowed his eyes at Peter's choice of words. None of his people had reported seeing any of them. But Graham had no doubt that Tess had reached out and made contact with Peter. But there was no point in trying to break Peter. There were certain men that would not break unless extreme measures were taken, not when it came to family. And Peter was one of them. Graham didn't have time, though, for extreme measures.

But that wouldn't be necessary. Graham took a seat in the chair in front of the desk. "I have a message that I want to be sent out to all Seraph Force Rangers. I will wait at Heaven's Field for Addison this afternoon. She will meet me, and the warrants for her compatriots will be canceled. If not, I will change the order to have them all killed on sight."

CHAPTER 55

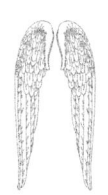

ADDIE

My head swam. He was back. I pictured him lying on the ground, his blood seeping into the ground below him. My own blood had dripped onto the ground below me. I thought he might not make it.

I had hoped that maybe, just maybe, with the injury he had received, he would have been jolted out of this angelic quest.

But nothing had changed.

"He's not Graham," Peter said, bewilderment in his tone. "I don't understand what's going on with him. He's cold. He didn't ask about any of the preparations in the city or the increase in the demon attacks. He showed no inkling of concern for anything except for …" He glanced over at me.

Donovan cursed softly. He turned for the door. "Well, our decision's made, then. You two grab what you need. We'll be leaving in ten minutes."

"No."

My response stopped him where he was. He turned back, slowly raising an eyebrow. "What do you mean 'no'?"

I took a deep breath, straightening my shoulders as a calm fell over me now that the decision had been made. "Graham's not going to stop. He's going to keep hunting me. And the longer he hunts me, the longer everyone else is in danger."

Donovan crossed his arms over his chest. "We can handle it. And we'll keep the kids—"

"It's not just about you guys, not anymore. D'Angelo's rules are endangering people across the nation. And with the demon attacks increasing, us going on the run takes fighters off the board that could be saving lives. Every day we run, every day we hide from Graham, is a day where people die. And for what? To keep me alive? It's not right."

"None of this is right. But that doesn't mean you need to face him," Donovan bit out before taking a deep breath. He looked at Tess. "You tell her."

Tess shook her head. "It's Addie's decision to make. And I support her either way."

Donovan's mouth dropped. "You—" He slammed his mouth shut, turning back to Addie. "What are you going to do? Are you going to kill him?"

I took a shuddering breath, picturing Graham's face, his dark eyes lighting up with happiness. Then I pictured the people I had come across, the ones that I'd been too late to save.

"Yes."

CHAPTER 56

Leaving the house without Tess or Donovan noticing would be impossible. After Peter left, they would watch me like hawks, waiting for me to make a break for the door. I agreed to wait until tomorrow, to think on it for a little while.

But it was all I'd been thinking about for the last few weeks. And I was done running.

Peter was torn about what to do about Graham and not sure what the best approach was, but he didn't offer any alternative solutions, and he promised not to say anything to Graham.

The truth was, there weren't any alternative possibilities. Graham died or I died, that was simply how it had to be. And I couldn't let it be me. The fact was that I could save more people than Graham could. And in the coming war, they were going to need me.

Which meant that Graham had to die.

My heart rebelled against the idea, but my head knew that it was right. For whatever reason, the archangel had set Graham on this path. But I didn't have to offer myself up as a lamb to slaughter. I didn't deserve that. Graham didn't deserve it either. Yet this was where we were.

Tess, Donovan, and I had stayed outside talking after Peter left. He needed to get back before his absence raised suspicion. Donovan argued against my going. He argued again for us to escape, but Tess stayed quiet.

Now she was in the kitchen making an early dinner. None of us had much of an appetite. So far the kids didn't know Graham was back, and I planned to keep it that way as long as possible.

I stepped back inside as Noel and Micah hurried down the stairs, bags in their hands. "Addie?"

I forced a smile to my face. "Hey."

"Everything okay?"

I nodded. "Yeah. Peter just wanted to give us an update on the demon attacks and let us know there'd been more reports of them targeting more isolated locations."

"So we're not leaving?" Noel asked.

"No, not yet. But just keep everything ready just in case, okay?"

"Okay. I've got to tell Torr. He's getting the horses ready." She dropped the bags against the wall and then disappeared down the hall.

Micah sniffed the air. "Smells like we're having pasta again."

"That it does. You should go see if Tess needs some help."

Donovan waited until Micah was out of earshot. "You're not going to tell them?"

"Not until I have to."

"You can't do this, Addie."

"I don't *want* to do this. But it's time."

I walked down the hall, a little annoyed at Donovan. I knew he was just trying to protect me. I knew he was worried about the kids and what would happen if something happened to me. But this was the best decision. This had to end. We'd been on the run for weeks, and here we were, right back at the same spot. Except

DEMON REVEALED

now more people were getting hurt. There wasn't a choice. I needed to face Graham. I needed to finish this.

As I stepped into the kitchen, Tess was putting pasta into bowls, then pouring sauce on top. Micah then took the bowls and placed them on the table. Donovan, Torr, and Noel showed up, taking their seats. I went to go sit down when Tess called me over. "Addie? Can you help me with something?"

"Sure." I stood back up. I walked over to the counter. "What do you need?"

"In the back of the root cellar, I think there's a big round of cheese. I discovered it earlier today. Can you go down there and grab it?"

I gave her a strange look. I hadn't noticed anything like that down there, but I shrugged. "Sure. Be right back."

I walked into the pantry and pulled open the trap door to the root cellar. After climbing down the ladder, I made my way toward the back. The root cellar had a dirt floor and dirt walls, except for one rock wall. Shelves had been placed along two of the walls, and some niches had been carved into the rock wall along the back. I stood in the middle, looking around, but saw nothing that resembled a block of cheese. "I don't see it," I yelled up to Tess.

"Along the back. At the end of the wooden shelf by the wall."

I frowned but turned back to the shelves and made my way along them. I checked each of the shelves that touched the exterior walls, but there was nothing here. There were some bags of potatoes, more pasta than any of us could use, some canned fruit and vegetables, but there was definitely no cheese. What was Tess talking about?

Shaking my head, I climbed back up the ladder. I walked out of the pantry. "Tess, I can't find it any—"

I stopped short. Donovan, Noel, Micah, and Torr all sat slumped at the table, their eyes closed. Tess bustled in from the hall, pillows in her arms. She started placing them under their heads.

"What on earth is going on?"

Tess pulled Micah's head down gently and then placed a pillow underneath it. "Vera gave me some of her knockout meds. She thought they might come in handy. Looks like she was right."

"But why?"

Tess carefully arranged a pillow under Torr's head. "I know you're going to face Graham. And if it were me, once the decision was made, I'd want to get it over with. And you know as well as I do that every single person at this table will follow you, no matter the cost to them. This is the only way I could think of to keep them safe."

"What about you?"

Tess's mouth straightened into a line. "I don't want you to go either. I don't want you to have to face Graham. I don't want to face the reality that I'm going to lose one or both of you." Her chin trembled. She took a deep breath. "But I agree with you. This has to end. He's not going to stop. And you're right. More people are just going to continue to die. I hate that it's come to this, but this is where we're at."

I took my own deep breath, glancing out the window. "How far is that field from here?"

"Only about thirty minutes by horse. I'll go with you. It won't be dark for hours, so they'll be fine. Plus, the drugs should wear off in about an hour. And I think ..." She took a deep breath. "And I think someone should be there. For both of you."

I nodded, my chest feeling tight. "Thank you, Tess."

"When do you want to leave?"

I looked at my family sleeping at the table. I ran a hand over Micah's head and then kissed his cheek. It was never easy to leave. Whether the goodbyes were long or short, they would never be enough.

"Now."

CHAPTER 57

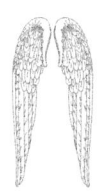

THE RIDE to the field was surprisingly peaceful. We rode through some beautiful country. At one point, Tess took us through a dormant fruit orchard.

"I used to sneak over here with Peter after the trees were in bloom, and we'd steal apples. We got chased by the orchard's owner a few times, but I could tell his heart wasn't really in it. I think he kind of liked that we were sneaking in."

"What makes you think that?"

Tess grinned at me. "After the first time he caught us, there was always a ladder propped up on one of the first trees. I think to make sure that we could get up into the trees safely."

I smiled at the idea of it.

Tess's smile turned wistful. "I wonder whatever happened to him."

We didn't speak for the rest of the journey. Ten minutes later, Tess put out a hand, pointing to the ridge ahead.

"Just over that ridge is the field. If Graham was being honest, he'll be waiting for you there. If he hasn't lured you into a trap." Tess glanced around.

"No, there's no trap," I said softly.

This was what the archangel wanted: a battle. And he wouldn't be cheated out of it by some trick. He wanted Graham and me to face one another. He wanted us to stare each other down and then fight to the death.

My stomach twisted at the thought of it, but my resolve hardened. This was a fight I couldn't lose.

A light appeared in the sky. My eyes jolted toward it. It streaked across the sky, heading for the field.

Tess mouth hung open. "Is that …"

I couldn't tear my gaze away from the light until it disappeared behind the ridge. But once again, there was no explosion. "Yes. That's the archangel Michael."

CHAPTER 58

I DISMOUNTED my horse before we reached the ridge and handed the reins to Tess.

Her hands wrapped around the reins. "I'll be nearby."

"Don't interfere, Tess. No matter what happens, don't interfere."

Tess stared down at me, tears causing her eyes to shine brightly. She gave me an abrupt nod and then pulled on the reins of my horse and slowly headed away.

I watched until she had disappeared from view. She would keep her word. It would kill her to do so, but she would keep her word.

I straightened my shoulders and turned toward the ridge. I walked slowly toward it, my nervousness fading. There was nothing to be nervous about. What would happen would happen. My nerves would only increase the likelihood of it being a bad outcome.

I nearly snorted at the thought. As if there could actually be a good outcome from this situation. As I cleared the rise, I saw two men standing in the middle of the clearing. The archangel stood with the same almost-golden light around him, as if demanding that even the light itself focus only on him.

But my gaze skipped over him in a second, drawn to the only person I wanted to see.

Graham stood a few feet in front of the archangel, his legs braced, his arms behind his back. He looked so strong. So determined.

So heartbreakingly handsome.

His skin had tanned from his time in the sun, and his white fitted shirt accentuated his muscular arms.

I flashed on falling into those arms at the Uriels' home. It felt like a lifetime ago. I remembered the feel of those arms around me, the feel of those warm lips on mine.

I searched his face for any sign of the Graham I knew. But the man who stared back at me showed no glimmer of him. He watched me coldly, assessing me as I walked toward him, mocking my memories. But the coldness served a purpose: It steeled my resolve. Because his gaze reminded me of the Graham I'd fought in Pitkin.

The Graham who tried to kill me. He failed then. He would fail now.

I stopped when I was about eight feet away. "I heard you were looking for me."

Graham nodded, pulling his sword from its sheath. I recognized the sword. It was the demon sword that I had given to Marcus. "It's time to finish this."

The demon sword erupted into flame.

I stumbled back, my eyes growing large. Graham charged.

CHAPTER 59

I DARTED up into the air, out of his reach. I knew this was the moment, but still I needed to try one more time. "Don't make me do this, Graham."

He didn't say anything. He simply stared at me with that stony expression.

Then wings sprouted from his back.

I gaped at him, my mouth hanging open. "How?"

Graham's only answer was to charge into the air at me.

My shock was so great that I barely managed to get my sword in front of me.

Graham had *wings*. The archangel had gifted him with wings. Neither Vera nor the books mentioned that as a possibility.

The crash of our swords rang out across the valley. He pressed toward me. I shifted to the side, knowing he wasn't used to fighting with wings. He hurtled past me, looking like he was stumbling on air.

I whirled around. His back was exposed to me.

It was the perfect moment. But I hesitated.

Then the moment was gone. Graham whirled around, coming back at me with ferocious intent. I bolted straight up, out of his reach. It took him a moment to switch directions and follow. He raced toward me.

I led him on a chase through the air, ducking and diving. He was slower, more awkward with the turns. But with each move, he grew stronger, more agile.

I broke away from him, hovering in the air. "Don't do this, Graham."

He slowly rose until he was only ten feet away. He was about to reply when his mouth froze halfway open. Emotions flashed across his face.

Hope burst through me. "Graham?"

With a roar, he charged at me, his sword leading the way.

On instinct, my own sword flew up to my defense. I surged back, but Graham was moving too fast. I readied for the impact.

But the clang of steel meeting steel didn't ring out. Instead, I felt the give of flesh as my sword pierced through Graham's stomach. I gasped, my eyes dropping to follow his sword as it fell to the ground. "No!"

Graham, *my* Graham, looked into my eyes as his blood seeped across the handle. "It was the only way," he whispered.

He placed his hands over mine, and with a violent tug, ripped my sword from my grasp. It was like his strings had been cut. He plummeted to the ground.

Bile rose up into my throat as I raced after him. But I wasn't fast enough. He slammed into the ground and rolled onto his side, the action freeing my sword.

I dropped to the ground ten feet away from him and walked slowly forward. His eyes were closed, his mouth a grimace of pain.

"Graham?"

His eyes slowly opened. Pain, anguish, and guilt stared back at me.

"Graham!" I bolted forward, dropping to my knees next to him. "I'm sorry. I'm so sorry."

He shook his head, reaching out for my hands. His voice was soft, weak. "No. You did the right thing. You had no choice. I would have killed you."

Tears rolled down my cheeks. "We'll get you to a doctor. You'll be fine."

Graham shook his head. Sweat covered his brow, and his lips were pale. "No. If you heal me, I'll just come back for you again and again. You need to let me go."

"I can't do that."

Strained lines appeared around Graham's eyes. Pain laced his voice. "Please, Addie."

Movement from my right pulled my attention. I jerked my head up as the archangel Michael strode toward us. I'd completely forgotten he was there, my attention solely locked on Graham.

"Get up," Michael barked. "I order you to get up!"

Graham just closed his eyes.

"This is what is wrong with humans: You're weak. Good for nothing. One simple task: kill the half-breed, and you couldn't even accomplish that." A sword appeared in Michael's hand, pulsing with light. "I guess I'll have to take care of it myself."

CHAPTER 60

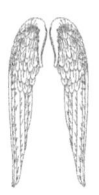

MICHAEL WAS a vision of death stepping right out of one of the books I'd read in Vera's library. This was the warrior angel of God.

And he was coming for me.

"Go, get out of here. Go." Graham pushed against my arm.

I stumbled to my feet, grabbing my sword as I backed away from Graham.

But Michael didn't change directions. He headed straight for Graham, a wicked smile on his face. "You humans and your useless emotions." He raised his sword.

"No!" I dashed forward to meet his blade. My blade slipped in front of his, keeping him from running Graham through. Energy burst from my own sword, shoving Michael back ten feet. He landed in a crouch.

I stood in front of Graham, my sword clasped in front of me with both hands. "You don't get to touch him."

Michael got to his feet. His eyes narrowed to slits. "You will pay for that."

I felt the energy welling up inside of me again. I glared at the archangel who had destroyed my life. Who had destroyed

Graham's. And for what? I still didn't know what any of this was about.

But I was done feeling guilty.

I held out my left hand. A ball of fire appeared in it. I hurled it forward.

Michael dodged to the side. The edge of his tunic came away singed. Energy ball after energy ball appeared in my hands as I stalked after the archangel. I lobbed them at him, pushing him back, away from Graham.

That was my only goal.

I had no illusions that I would be able to survive a fight with Michael. But I needed to get him far enough away from Graham that he might survive.

I hurled another fireball. Michael dodged to the left. He brought up his sword and swatted it away. "Enough!"

The whole ground seemed to tremble at his shout.

Or maybe it was just my own knees turning to jelly.

He advanced on me so incredibly fast that I barely managed to get my sword up in time. And this time I was the one who stumbled back. He came at me with strike after strike. Each one shoved me back farther and farther. The vibration of each one shook down my arms until they were practically numb. I struggled to keep my grip on my sword, knowing that if I lost it, this fight was over.

He swung again with a roar. The blow sent me flying into the air. I landed with a heavy thud. The air burst out from my lungs, and I struggled to breathe.

But worse, my sword rolled from my hand.

I stared up at Michael, my arms wide, my mouth gaping open, knowing that this was the moment I was going to die.

CHAPTER 61

MICHAEL STRODE TOWARD ME, but he was not the archangel I had first seen. His anger made what I had once thought was a most beautiful face hideous.

From the corner of my eye, I saw a bolt of light stream down from the sky. Was I hallucinating? Or maybe one of Michael's brothers in arms had come to watch his final destruction of the half-breed. The light grew closer, but Michael didn't seem to notice. He was too intent on me as he pulled back his arm, ready to let go with a slashing blow. He released his arm.

I closed my eyes as I tensed, waiting for the pain.

A crash of metal rang out.

I cracked open my eyes. A sword glowed two inches from my face, keeping Michael's sword from reaching me. The wielder of the sword pushed Michael away and then stepped next to me.

Vera braced her legs, her gray wings spread out behind her as she stood defiantly in front of me. "You don't get this one, brother."

CHAPTER 62

I SCRAMBLED TO MY FEET, grabbing my sword and moving next to her. I didn't know where she'd come from or how she'd found us, but I knew she was no match for Michael. "Vera, get out of here. He'll kill you."

Vera shook her head, not taking her gaze from Michael. "It's okay, Addie. I've got this."

Michael laughed, getting to his feet. "So you finally came out of hiding. Tell me, Gabriel, how has your human life been?"

"It's everything I could have wanted and more."

I gaped. "Gabriel?"

Michael straightened, staring at Vera. He scoffed. "Look what's become of you. You're an old woman."

"Appearances mean nothing. You know that. But if it makes you feel better …" Light shimmered over her. When it disappeared, the woman I had come to know was gone. In her place stood a strong, striking tall redhead with flashing green eyes. Her body was encased in a suit of armor made of silver, and her wings, instead of a dull gray, were a brilliant white with shades of pink along the edges.

"You need to leave this place, Michael," Vera said.

"I'm not leaving."

Vera sighed. "I'd hoped after all these years that your anger would have lessened. That you would have begun to understand the humans and why they are important."

"They are not important. They never have been."

Vera turned only slightly, keeping one eye on Michael while she spoke with me. "Get him out of here."

Then with a yell, she charged at Michael.

CHAPTER 63

I COULD BARELY PULL my gaze from the archangels as they fought in the sky above me. Every time their swords met, the sound rang out across the valley, cutting through my body with a tremble. I scrambled back to Graham. After only a moment's hesitation, I dropped my sword and yanked my jacket off, pushing it against the wound in his stomach.

"No. Go, Addie. Get out of here."

"Not without you," I said while trying to figure out how I was going to carry him while keeping the jacket in place.

The sound of hooves striking the ground caused my head to jerk up. Tess dropped to the ground from her horse, grabbing the pack that had been tied to the back of the saddle as she did so. She hurried over to the two of us.

"I thought I told you to stay away," I said.

Tess shrugged as she rifled through the pack. "I'm not great at taking orders. You should ask him about that."

Graham let out a sigh, closing his eyes. "She's really not."

I didn't know how the two of them could joke at a time like this. All I could do was stare at Graham's blood seeping into the ground. "It's bad. My sword went right into his stomach."

Tess pulled out bandages, and I quickly removed the jacket. "What now?" I asked.

"We need to get him up."

I pulled him into a sitting position. Graham winced and let out a little grunt in response.

Then Tess started wrapping the strips around him, glancing at the two archangels still locked in battle in the skies above us. Her mouth dropped open slightly and her eyes widened. "Is that Vera?"

"Yeah, but I think she might be the archangel Gabriel."

Tess stared at me for a moment and then back to the task at hand. "Well, okay."

A scream sounded from the sky. All three of us looked up. Michael held his side, his sword's light growing dimmer as Vera hovered in the air a few feet away from him. I couldn't hear what she said, but a few seconds later, Michael flew back into the sky. He was gone.

Vera hovered there for a few more seconds, watching the empty sky before she flew back down to the ground and landed next to us. "How is he?"

"Not great. We need to stitch him up."

Vera shook her head. "There's no time for that. Roll him onto his back. Remove the bandages."

We did as ordered.

She looked at Graham. "This is going to hurt."

He nodded, closing his eyes and balling his hands into fists. Vera's sword caught fire again, and she placed it on his wound. Graham screamed.

I turned my head, not able to watch. But then he quieted. I turned back, and Vera nodded. "That will stop the bleeding. And the swords heat will actually accentuate the healing."

"Seriously?" Tess asked.

"It's a little perk of the angel blades."

I stared at her still, trying to accept the fact that the woman standing in front of me was Vera. "What just happened?"

Vera sighed, looking off into the sky. "You just got caught in a family feud. Let's go somewhere more comfortable, and then I'll explain."

I was desperate to ask her more questions, but Graham was the priority now, so the questions would have to wait. They were practically burning the tip of my tongue. But instead of a question, I started with the most pressing thought in my mind. "Thank you for saving us."

Vera glanced back at me before turning again to the sky. "Don't thank me yet. I may have just made things worse for all of you."

"Worse than this?" Tess indicated Graham.

Vera gave a grim nod. "Yes."

CHAPTER 64

I COULDN'T SEEM to pull my gaze from Vera. She looked so strong, so young. And she was the archangel Gabriel. Then in a flash, she shifted back to the Vera we all knew. She smiled at my expression with a shrug. "I prefer this appearance. I've earned it."

I had a million questions for her. But someone had to have seen those bolts of light. And possibly heard her and Michael fighting. Which meant we needed to move quickly.

I helped Graham get up onto one of the horses and then mounted the horse in front of him. He looked like hell, but he was definitely in better shape than before Vera had cauterized the wound. Graham looked over at Tess, who'd just settled on her horse. "Get Peter. We need to know what's going on. We need to figure out ... next steps."

Tess hesitated, her gaze meeting mine.

I turned around to look into Graham's face, and it was *Graham's* face. He smiled at me, even though I could tell he was still in pain. "It's okay. It's just me now. That darkness is gone."

Vera nodded, hovering in the air between us. "Michael's done with you. His hold is broken. You were able to pull away from him, weren't you?"

Graham grinned at her. "Someone suggested that that might be possible. And I focused on that."

Vera let out a cackling laugh. "Good boy."

I nodded at Tess. "Get word to Peter. But be careful."

A brief nod was all Tess gave me before she took off at a bolt. Vera and I headed for the cottage.

I rode as fast as I dared, still worried about Graham. But he held my waist tightly, not showing any sign he was in danger of falling off.

The warmth of him against my back was making me a little light-headed.

I focused on getting us home, but I couldn't help but replay Vera's words in my mind.

His hold is broken.

Was it true? Was Graham now back to himself? I wanted to believe it more than anything, but at the same time, I didn't want to get my hopes up. But the longer we rode with his body pressed against mine, the more I realized that was a battle I had already lost.

The cottage was quiet as we approached, but then the front door swung open. Donovan stood there, taking up the doorway. The fact that he stood there and didn't charge outside showed that he wasn't quite back to normal yet.

Even from this distance, I could see him blinking hard as he stared at the incoming horses, trying to figure out who was who. But then his face arranged into concern as he caught sight of Graham.

I just hoped he didn't attack first and ask questions later.

Donovan disappeared back into the doorway. Graham leaned forward, his lips nearly touching my ear. "How's he going to react to seeing me?" he asked.

I shivered at his closeness and tried to focus only on his question.

It wasn't easy. Despite what we had just been through, and

despite the fact that Graham was injured and everything that had happened between us, feeling his body so close to mine was doing all sorts of things to my mind and my body.

But now was most definitely not the time to explore that.

"I don't know," I murmured. "But hopefully he'll give us a chance to explain."

By the time we reached the fence, Noel and Torr were outside with Donovan. They had moved to the middle of the courtyard. And all of them stood there armed. Vera flew into the courtyard first, with me and Graham right behind her.

We pulled to a stop only a few feet away from them.

Donovan looked from Vera to Graham. His eyebrows raising as Vera retracted her wings. "What's going on?"

"Quite a bit, actually." Vera nodded toward the swords along Donovan's back. "You won't be needing those, at least not for Graham. Michael's gift has been removed. He's back to his normal self."

Donovan didn't look even slightly convinced. "And how can you be so sure?"

Vera gave him a smile. "Let's just say I have the inside track on how the archangels' abilities work."

I could see the hope in Donovan's eyes but also the wariness. He wanted to believe Vera. *I* wanted to believe Vera. But none of us were sure whether or not we should.

Once I was on the ground, I turned to help Graham. His face was filled with pain. And as he lowered himself to the ground, his legs shook for minute.

"We need to get you inside, and maybe get you something to eat or drink."

Graham swallowed, licking his lips, which were awfully pale. "I wouldn't say no to a little water."

I studied his face, wanting so hard to believe that he was truly back with us. "Do you feel different?"

Graham nodded, one hand on the saddle of the horse to keep

himself upright. "The last few times I came back to myself, I could always feel this presence in the back of my mind. It was smallest when I was in Pitkin recovering."

"That's because I was keeping you covered," said Vera. "I kept you hidden from Michael. He wasn't able to sense you while you were under my wing, so to speak. I also nudged this one"—she smiled at Noel—"so that she would know where Addie was."

Noel let out a little gasp. "That morning. I knew we had to continue east. That we shouldn't head north just yet."

"It was a small manipulation, but I knew your family had to be back together. You are stronger together. And with you all in one spot, it was easier for me to keep Michael from knowing where you were."

"Wait, wait, how were you able to keep people hidden from an archangel?" Donovan asked.

"Because I used to go by a different name. I was called Gabriel, the archangel. But I haven't gone by that name for the last hundred or so years."

In a burst of light, the Vera we knew was gone, replaced by the warrior I had seen in the field. Noel and Torr stumbled back, their eyes going wide. Donovan just stood with his arms crossed over his chest, the slight tick in his cheek the only indication that he was affected by Vera's transformation. After a moment, Vera switched back to the more common version, to the face we had grown used to.

Vera shrugged. "I've been living on Earth for the last ten decades. I wanted to see what all the fuss was about. I have to say, I understand now why so many wanted a chance at this life. Even with all the heartache and the difficulty, it is a good one."

Donovan ran a hand through his hair. "So you really are an archangel?"

Vera nodded. "That I am. And Graham here needs to lie down before he falls down."

Donovan looked at Graham. Distrust and hope warred for

dominance on his face.

I met Donovan's gaze. "Let's get him inside and into bed. He's wounded. We'll keep an eye on him and make sure he's truly back to normal."

"Oh, he is," Vera said. "He refused Michael's gift. When ordered to kill you, he tried to sacrifice himself instead. It broke the command. It's one of the unfortunate side effects of trying to control humans. That pesky free will of yours."

Vera walked over and slipped an arm around Graham's waist. After a moment's hesitation, Donovan walked over and slipped an arm around the other side. "I'll help."

The two of them walked him into the house. I turned to Noel and Torr.

Noel crossed her arms over her chest. "You left us again."

I sighed. "Well, yes, but Tess was one who drugged you. I didn't know about that. But I came back. There are just some battles you guys can't fight with me. But I will always come back."

Noel's shoulders dropped along with her arms. She walked over and hugged me tight. "You're okay, right?"

I leaned my head against her, hugging her back. "I'm not hurt. But Graham ... what Vera said was true. Graham and I were fighting, and then all of a sudden he put himself in front of my sword. I didn't realize what happened until my sword went through him. He disobeyed Michael's order."

"So he's back?" Torr asked.

"I hope so. But being none of us have dealt with this before, I can't say for sure. Where's Micah?"

Noel grinned. "When we saw the horses, we sent him in the back. He's getting a little tired of constantly being left out of the action."

"Well, let's go get him." I stepped toward the door.

Vera stepped out of the doorway before I reached it. She looked at the three of us. "Actually, I need to speak with Addie alone for a little bit first."

CHAPTER 65

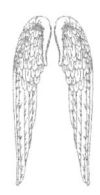

NOEL AND TORR went inside to check on Graham and Micah. I knew that they would also be setting up a guard so that Graham was never alone in case he changed back into that cold monster.

But I was putting faith in what Vera had said. She and I, instead of going back inside, headed around the side of the house, taking the horses to the stable. We got them some water and some hay and wiped them down. Then the two of us sat in the stable on opposite sides of the barn path. I studied her. She still looked like the same Vera. Her gray hair sprinkled with strands of white was pulled back into a long braid. Her green eyes shone out of a well-lived face. "So you're really the archangel Gabriel?"

Vera inclined her head. "At your service."

"Are there more archangels around on ... angel sabbatical?"

Vera gave a cackling laugh. "It's possible. After the war, I knew I needed to step back. I'd been around humans for a long time by that point. It was the first time any of us had been exposed to them on a regular basis. And some of us were a little more susceptible to your charms.

"You see, an archangel's life is all about duty and nothing else. But you humans, you are so much more than what we'd been told.

It was explained to us about your emotions and the lives that you led, but it was the difference between reading the words in a cold book and seeing it up close and personal.

"Your joy, it was a mystery to me at first. You find happiness in the simplest of things. You could find laughter even when the world is at its lowest point; I hadn't expected that. I went into the war convinced of the rightness of our actions: Lucifer and his minions were wrong. And it was our duty to set things right. Truth be told, it was less about the demons plaguing humanity and more about showing Lucifer that we were stronger than he was."

Vera shook her head, grabbing a handful of dirt and tossing it down the stable alley. "But then I watched as humans sacrificed themselves to save the ones they loved. Or sometimes to save a stranger.

"And then there were the children. I had never seen children before. And yet these adults were running around doing everything in their power to keep them safe. These little, tiny beings were completely powerless and yet so very powerful at the same time. I didn't understand it."

"So what changed?" I asked.

Vera shrugged. "I don't think there was any one particular incident. It was a combination of so many. And without even realizing it, I began to fight not to prove Lucifer wrong, but to keep the humans safe. I didn't recognize that it was happening at first. It was just this slow creep over me. I started taking more risks, taking on more and more missions. And when the war was over and we succeeded, the idea of going back to that cold existence without emotions, without laughter …" She shook her head. "I couldn't do it. I wasn't ready to renounce my place on high, but I wasn't ready to go back either. So I asked and was granted time. And so I have been on this planet for over a hundred years."

"And you were married to a human."

Vera smiled. "Reginald was such a good man. His mother used

to say he was always looking for a laugh. Before him, I wandered, spending time in different towns, getting to know different people, but when I met Reginald and his family, I decided to stay. And I decided to let myself age so that I could."

"Did he know who you were?"

Vera shook her head. "No. It would only have placed him in danger to know. It would have been a secret, a burden he would have had to carry. I didn't want to add that to his life. If he needed to know, if his life or anyone's were put in danger because of my presence, I would have told him. But he never did need to know. We lived a good life. And I got to have a son." Vera's eyes were bright with tears. "I wouldn't trade those experiences for anything."

"And now?"

She sighed. "Now I'm not sure what the next steps are. I don't believe my brothers and sisters in arms knew I was on Earth. But now that they do, well, let's just say I don't think it's going to be the last that I've seen of them."

A burst of thunder rumbled from the sky. Vera jolted, her eyes narrowing as she quickly got to her feet and strode to the barn entrance.

I stumbled to my feet a little more slowly as my heart pounded. I knew that sound.

I reached Vera's side in the open doorway of the stable. In the distance, bolts of lightning streaked toward the ground. I counted at least five. I couldn't tell how far away they were, but they came from the same direction as the field where Michael had been.

Vera swore softly. "I had hoped I would have more time."

"We need to get everybody. We need to move."

Vera grabbed my arm as I tried to rush past, holding me in place. "They're not here for you. This time, they've come for me."

The archangels are after Vera now but it doesn't mean they've forgotten about Addie or Graham. The story continues in Demon Heir.

Sign up here for the newsletter and be the first hear *Demon Cursed* news. Plus get the newsletter and exclusive content.

It's good to be in the know . . .

Continue Reading for a Peek at the third book in *The Demon Cursed* Series

SNEAK PEEK AT DEMON HEIR

ADDIE

The bolts of lightning could be seen clearly, even though they hit the ground in the distance. I didn't have to be there to know where they landed: Heaven's Field. The field where Graham and I fought. The field where the archangel Michael had watched, waiting to see my blood spilled, waiting to see the commander of the Seraph Force take my life.

But the archangel's plan hadn't gone as he'd hoped, and all because of the archangel standing next to me: Vera, also known as Gabriel. Vera, her white hair pulled back in a long thick braid, stood with one wrinkled hand on the large doorframe of the barn. Her green eyes were fixed on the four shapes that appeared in the sky near the field.

My heart in my throat, I knew it was Michael returning, this time with reinforcements. Graham and I had survived thanks to Vera's intervention. But against these odds, not even Vera would be enough.

"We need to warn the others." I took a step forward.

Vera grabbed my hand, stopping me. "There's no need. I'll lead them away."

"They're not here for you, Vera. I'm the daughter of Lucifer. They want me dead."

Shaking her head slowly, Vera dropped my hand. "That's no longer their top priority. I broke the cardinal rule: I took up arms against my brother. That cannot be allowed to stand. It might give the others some ideas. I will be caught and tried for that." She gave a short laugh. "It will be a very short trial."

I stared at her, my heart breaking. After all this time, she'd come out of hiding to save Graham, to save me. She'd been contentedly locked away in Pitkin with her library and animals until Torr and I stumbled in, blowing apart her life.

"I'm sorry, Vera. This is all my fault. If I—"

She turned to face me. "Now you listen here. This confrontation has been a long

time coming. And I knew the consequences of throwing in with you. I chose this fight. I should have chosen it a long time ago. I should have defended humans more during the Angel Wars. Perhaps I could have saved more."

"Wouldn't Michael have just come for you earlier?"

She shrugged. "Probably. But maybe I could have convinced my brothers and sisters to join me, at least some of them. Now, they might not even know I'm gone."

"What can I do?"

"There's nothing for you to do. Michael is not interested in Graham any longer. But he *is* still interested in you. But I will be the bigger priority for the moment. It will give you time." She glanced toward where the lightning had struck. The shapes had grown larger. They were coming.

Vera pulled my attention back to her, her eyes intense. "You need to find your father. He's the only one who can help you now."

"I-I don't know where he is. I don't know how to find him."

Vera cupped my face in her hand. "Yes, you do. You only need to remember."

I shot my gaze to the approaching figures. "Are you going to be all right?" She had done so much for us. I couldn't bear the idea of her being killed for those actions.

Vera grinned as her wings popped out from behind her. "I'll be fine. I know this world better than they do. I'll take them on a nice long chase, and then I'll hide out where they can't find me. It will buy you some time."

"But will you be able to escape?"

For the first time, I saw sadness in Vera's gaze. "They will hunt me until they have found me, no matter how long it takes. I'm sure eventually they will succeed. But I won't make it easy for them."

Donovan, Torr, Noel, and Graham burst from the house. Their eyes focused on approaching threat.

Even from here, I could see the archangels' wings beating furiously as they headed toward us.

Vera gripped both of my wrists, demanding my attention again. "Don't worry about me. Just find your father. He's the one you need now. As for my brother, tell him I'm sorry. I didn't understand." She leaned forward and kissed me on the forehead.

A tear escaped my eyes and rolled down my cheek.

Vera gave me a soft smile as she pulled back, her eyes bright with unshed tears. "See? That's what's so great about humans. How quickly you come to care for one another." She squeezed my hands again and then took off into the sky, hovering above the barn, waiting to make sure the archangels caught sight of her. Then, with one last wave at the others, she increased her speed until she was only a burst of light careening through the sky.

The other archangels were close enough to see now. Michael was in the lead, the three others flying behind him. Their eyes tracked the trail of light that was Vera.

One by one, they shifted, save for one. He paused, hovering in the air, staring straight at me. My breath caught at the anger on his face.

I tensed, my own wings flinging out behind me. I would have to lead him away, give the others time to escape. I took a step forward, my wings lighting with flames.

The archangel's expression shifted from anger to uneasiness. With one last glare, he sped after the others. As a group they shifted to a speed beyond the capability of human eyes to see. They too shifted to no more than trails of light in the sky. The anger on the one that had slowed flowed through my mind. Why had he stopped? Was he angry Vera had helped us? But it had felt more personal than that.

I stayed where I was, watching until the light from their flight had completely faded.

And with it, the concerns about that one archangel's behavior. Instead, my thoughts focused solely on Vera. I rubbed my chest, which felt tight at the thought of the danger she was in.

Stay safe, Vera. And thank you.

GRAHAM

Lightning strikes and accompanying thunder shook the house. Donovan's and Graham's gazes met. "Archangels," Graham said.

Donovan stared at him before his gaze shifted to the windows and back, his whole body tense. "Are you truly back?" he demanded.

Graham nodded. "Whatever Michael did to me, it's gone. The last few times I woke up, I knew it was only a matter of time. But now it's gone."

Donovan stared at him, trying to read something in Graham's face. Finally, he nodded. "Well, I hope so, because if you stab me in the back, I'm going to be really ticked off. Let's go."

The two of them strode to the front door. Noel and Torr were already there. And Micah had appeared from his hiding spot.

Micah darted behind Torr as Graham's gaze fell upon him.

Graham's gut clenched. "I'm sorry, Micah. It wasn't me, not really."

Micah peeked out from behind Torr. "I know," he said, but he made no effort to move toward Graham.

Graham knew he had no right to ask for any more than that. Micah's words were more than he even expected.

"Is that the archangels?" Noel asked, looking outside.

Graham nodded. "I think so. But I have a feeling it's more than one. You three need to be ready to ride if it's as bad as we think. Donovan and I will hold them off the best we can. Go find Peter and Tess, okay?"

Noel met his gaze, and then flicked it over to Donovan, wanting conformation.

"He's right. If this goes badly, find Tess," Donovan said.

Noel finally nodded leading the other two to the back of the house.

Donovan and Graham stepped out of the front of the house. Graham's chest tightened as fear rolled over him as he noted the shapes in the sky moving toward them quickly. *My God, there are four of them.* He was already injured, which meant he wouldn't be much use in a fight. And whatever extra strength he'd gotten from Michael was gone as well.

He paused, thinking about the wings. He hadn't even known he'd had them until they'd sprung out behind him. He'd felt a heaviness under his skin when Michael arrived in the field. But now, that was gone too, and he was sure they were gone. Which was a pity, because he was pretty sure they would come in handy in the coming fight.

Anger rolled through him as he watched the angels draw closer. All his life, he'd learned about the archangels. All his life, he'd heard about their incredible feats. And yet those tales had left a great deal out. They'd left out the coldness, the heartlessness inherent within each angel. They were not creatures to be revered; they were creatures to be feared.

"You got this?" Donovan asked, keeping his gaze on the approaching threat.

"Yes."

Vera and Addie appeared in the stable doorway. They spoke intensely for a few moments, and then Vera burst into the air.

"What's she doing?" Donovan asked, his eyes growing large.

Graham shifted his gaze from Vera to the archangels, the truth hitting him. "She's making sure they see her."

Then Vera flew away so fast it was hard to track her. The archangels immediately gave chase. Although one stopped, staring at Addie. He only flew away when Addie stepped forward, her wings enflamed.

And Graham realized none of the other angels had flaming wings. Was that trait only Addie's? Or did Lucifer share the same ability?

Donovan stared up at the sky. "What just happened?"

Addie approached them, wiping at her eyes. "They aren't interested in us right now. They just want Vera. Apparently fighting against another angel is the worst thing you can possibly do. It's even worse than being the child of one."

The light trails in the sky had disappeared. And Graham felt completely helpless. Vera had saved his life twice now, once in Pitkin and once on the field. And now all he could do was hope she could fly fast.

"Does she have a plan?" Graham asked.

"She's going to lead them on a long chase, but she knows eventually they'll catch her." Addie's voice was calm with no inflection, but he saw the emotion on her face.

He wanted to comfort her, to offer her some words of hope. But he didn't have any, and he doubted she'd want them from him anyway.

"So, what do we do now?" Donovan asked.

"Vera said I need to find my father. That he's the only one who can help me now."

Graham clasped his hands behind his back to keep from reaching for her. "Did she say where we can find him?"

Addie shook her head. "No. She said that I'd know. All I needed to do was remember. But I can't remember anything before I woke up on that beach."

Donovan nodded toward the sky. "If that's what Vera said, then that's what we'll do. We'll get your memory back."

"And I promise, I will get you back to your father," Graham said.

Addie met his gaze. Graham's stomach clenched at the pain he saw there; pain he knew he was partially responsible for.

"But how?" she asked. "It's been two years. I don't remember a thing."

"We'll find someone who can help you," Graham said.

"Who can possibly help me with this?" Addie asked, sounding hopeless.

But Graham knew there was one person who might be able to aid them. "Marcus."

ADDIE

I stayed outside after the archangels disappeared, keeping watch. The others went inside to pack up our limited supplies.

Graham went too, even though there was nothing in the cottage belonging to him. He felt uncomfortable around me; that was obvious. He'd barely said anything to me. And even then, only when he had to, his words formal. But it wasn't the same coldness I saw in him in Pitkin and on the field. No, his eyes were different. They looked at me with guilt and regret.

But I didn't want that. I wanted to forget all of this and just have Graham back. On the ride here, I'd envisioned the possibilities of a future with Graham in it. Yes, it was a different future than what I'd first envisioned back in Sterling Peak, but it had one common element: Graham and I standing side by side facing it.

But now, that seemed so idealistic. Graham was no longer under Michael's control, but he remembered at least some of what he had done. I should have expected him to pull away, to beat himself up over events he had no control over.

Two riders on horseback appeared at the far end of the field.

I moved to the gate, squinting to get a better view of them. Peter and Tess raced toward the cottage.

Tess outpaced Peter. She pulled her horse to a sharp stop only a few feet from me. "What happened? Is everyone all right?"

Peter pulled to a stop next to her, his eyes scanning the cottage behind me. "Were those archangels?"

Suddenly, all that we had been through hit me. And all that we still had to do. Exhaustion fell over me. "Yes. And things may have gotten worse."

∼

After a quick conversation with Tess and Peter, it was agreed that we would immediately move over to Peter's home. It wasn't just for the better accommodations. We'd be leaving first thing in the morning, and Peter's home was a little farther south.

Plus, no one liked the idea of staying in a place the archangels knew.

When we arrived at Peter's, Seth, Peter's husband, was thrilled at our arrival. He hugged Tess tight, tsking over her appearance. He had us all sorted in guest rooms within a few minutes, without any advance notice of our arrival. Fresh clothes were sent up to each room with instructions to head to the dining room when we were ready.

I grabbed a shower first, luxuriating in the hot water. I climbed out regretfully, knowing Noel, Torr, and Micah were waiting.

When I ducked my head out, Micah was curled up asleep on the bed, a fresh shirt and linen pants on, his hair wet.

Noel moved away from the window, nodding toward Micah.

"Donovan let him use his shower. Torr's in there now. He said he'd head back when he was done. How was the shower?"

"Heaven,' I said before wincing at my choice of words.

Noel walked over and hugged me. I leaned my head on her shoulder. We were about the same height now. When we'd first met, she'd barely reached my shoulder. "Vera's going to be okay, right?"

I wanted to reassure her. I wanted to tell her that Vera would be fine. But I couldn't lie to her. "Vera's strong. She'll keep them chasing her for a good long time."

Her eyes, way too old for someone her age, locked on me. "And when they catch her?"

"Hopefully by then we'll have a way to help her."

"Are you really going to find your father?"

"Unless anyone has any better ideas, that seems our only option right now." I paused. "I can't fight him, Noel. I'm hoping Lucifer has some sort of weapon or something that I can use. If not…"

Noel bit her lips as if trying to keep her words back. But she didn't argue. Instead, she nodded. "Okay."

Then she slipped past me, shutting the bathroom door behind her.

I stared at the closed door for a long moment before making my way over to the bed and curling up next to Micah, clutching a pillow to my chest.

Vera's words rolled through my mind. *Find your father. He's the one you need now.*

I closed my eyes, wondering how adding the Devil to this situation could do anything but make it so much worse.

I fell asleep on the bed while waiting for Noel. When I awoke, Noel and Micah were fast asleep on the bed as well. Even Torr was snoring lightly, propped up in a chair next to the bed. I looked at each of them, my heart expanding. This was my family. And I would do whatever it took to keep them safe.

Even face the Devil himself.

***Demon Heir* is available on Amazon**

ABOUT THE AUTHOR

Sadie Hobbes is a dog lover, martial artist, avid runner, mother, wife, and Amazon best selling thriller writer under a different name. She can often be found before dawn wandering her yard with her dogs, dictating her latest novel. If anyone were to see her, they would seriously question her sanity as well as her fashion choices. (Think rain boots over pajamas plus a bulky cardigan). But it works for her!

If you'd like to hear about her upcoming releases, sign up for her newsletter through her facebook page.

She can be reached at sadiehobbesauthor@gmail.com or on her Facebook page.

ALSO BY SADIE HOBBES

The Demon Cursed Series

Demon Cursed

Demon Revealed

Demon Heir

The Four Kingdoms Series

Order of the Goddess

Copyright © 2020 by Sadie Hobbes

Demon Revealed

Published by Scottish Seoul Publishing, LLC, Dewitt, NY

All Rights Reserved. No part of this book may be reproduced or transmitted in any form or by any means, electronic or mechanical, including photocopying, recording, or by any information storage and retrieval system without the written permission of the author, except where permitted by law.

Printed in the United States of America.

Printed in Great Britain
by Amazon